The Comanchero's Grave

A Novel

Karen Kelling

The Comanchero's Grave

A Novel

Karen Kelling

SUNSTONE
PRESS

SANTA FE

Sunstone books may be purchased for educational, business, or sales promotional use.
For information please write: Special Markets Department, Sunstone Press,
P.O. Box 2321, Santa Fe, New Mexico 87504-2321.

Book and Cover design › Vicki Ahl
Body typeface › Bookman Old Style
Printed on acid-free paper

Library of Congress Cataloging-in-Publication Data

Kelling, Karen, 1947-
    The Comanchero's grave : a novel / by Karen Kelling.
        p. cm.
    ISBN 978-0-86534-861-5 (softcover : alk. paper)
    1. Granddaughters--Fiction. 2. Grandparents--Death--Fiction. 3. Inheritance and
succession--Fiction. 4. Ranch life--Texas--Fiction. 5. Texas--Fiction. I. Title.
    PS3611.E4437C66 2012
    813'.6--dc22

                                        2012002839

WWW.SUNSTONEPRESS.COM
SUNSTONE PRESS / POST OFFICE BOX 2321 / SANTA FE, NM 87504-2321 /USA
(505) 988-4418 / ORDERS ONLY (800) 243-5644 / FAX (505) 988-1025

To Curt,
Kim, Kat, Becky, Carmen,
the grandkids I've read to and the grandkids I've yet to read to.

PREFACE

I wished for a horse on every birthday candle and every first star I ever saw when I was growing up. When I went to college, I got a job and finally bought one. She was a beautiful palomino Quarter Horse named Tetrak Scootette, 334007. She was the only thing I owned when I got married—which was more than my poor husband owned, because he had to sell his horse to buy my wedding ring.

Since then, many of my wishes have come true. Some of the horses I wished for are in this book. I hope some of your horse wishes come true, too.

1

THE BULL SALE

Mary Lovella Grady wondered if the ranch dogs still waited on the back porch for Grampa Hank to come out and do chores. She did not see them as she and her mother came to a stop on the circular driveway in front of the imposing, main ranch house. Since Grampa Hank's funeral, the front porch of the two-story rock house had been taken over by tumbleweeds. They covered the front door and deep window sills full of pots that used to overflow with Granny's colorful flowers. Grampa Hank let the flowers die the previous summer after losing Granny, his wife of sixty years. Lovie was devastated she would never see Granny and Grampa Hank ever again.

The December wind was bitter and Lovie's long French braid did nothing to protect her ears when she stepped out of her mother's *Land Rover*. For the first time in her thirteen years, she did not want to spend Christmas vacation at the multigenerational Crossover Ranch—which Grampa Hank had promised to pass on to her one day.

Nothing had gone right for Lovie since her thirteenth birthday. She had refused to eat her usual orange and black birthday cake. Somehow turning thirteen-years-old on Halloween seemed like a bad omen. She was right. Two days after Halloween, the day some of her friends in Santa Fe celebrated the Day of the Dead, Grampa Hank was killed in a horseback accident.

Lovie's sadness at the loss of both of her grandparents morphed into angry outbursts aimed mostly at her mother. Today, Mrs. Grady welcomed the silent treatment from her daughter as they travelled from their mountain home east of Santa Fe, New Mexico, to the deserted Texas ranch.

Lovie broke her silence with ugly words as she fought her way through stickery, brown weed-balls to wheel her suitcase to the ornate, beveled-glass front door. But a smile sneaked onto her lips when the dogs, Dingo and Cotton, discovered her and smeared her nose and cheeks with slobbery kisses. The kisses froze to her face before her mother managed to yank her winter coat out from under boxes of groceries in the back seat of the *Land Rover*.

Dingo heard another vehicle approaching and bounded off the porch. A beat-up yellow van rounded the corner of the high courtyard wall connecting the main house with the cookhouse and bunkhouse behind. The van picked up speed when its occupants saw Mrs. Grady and it slung gravel at her. Determined to take chunks out of the van's tires, Dingo chased it down the long paved driveway, over the cattleguard and out the formerly grand entrance of the historic ranch headquarters.

"Dadgum. Who was that?" Lovie demanded.

"I believe that was our caretakers," Mrs. Grady muttered as she zipped up her coat, "or I should say our ex-caretakers. I hope they remembered to put a heat lamp in the well house to keep the pipes from freezing."

"I hope they put a heat lamp on the back porch to keep the dogs from freezing, especially Cotton. She's getting so old."

Mrs. Grady's cold fingers fumbled for the key to the front door. "Their letter said they intended to leave as soon as I got here. They didn't waste any time, did they? I wish they'd told me up front they were afraid to live this far out in the country instead of making up wild excuses to quit. We need all the help we can get this week. I suppose Dad told you they claimed the cookhouse is haunted. How pathetic. I almost feel sorry for them."

"I don't feel sorry for them, Mom. Dad told you they fried their brains in the sixties. He didn't want you to hire them in the first place, remember? You know they made up that story about seeing a wolf crawling out of the sunken grave by our family cemetery, the freaks. And they flat-out lied about the dogs keeping them awake all night howling at whatever it was. Grampa Hank told me Cotton hasn't howled since she got over losing her pups in that really bad ice storm that ruined Granny's orchard. And Dingo just howls when he's hungry."

"Dingo is always hungry, Lovie."

The ranch was no longer the cornucopia of dog scraps it had been when Granny kept a cook in the cookhouse to feed Grampa Hank's bunkhouse full of hungry cowboys. It hurt Lovie that nothing at the ranch would ever be the same as it was when Granny and Grampa Hank were alive. It was bad enough that finances forced her mother to replace all the resident ranch hands and their families with less expensive day workers. Then she announced she would have to hold a dispersal sale of all the cattle and horses to pay estate taxes.

Rumors spread that the ranch would be sold next. Hopeful real estate brokers sent poinsettias to the ranch with their business cards the day after Mrs. Grady and her angry daughter arrived to prepare for the dispersal sale.

The poinsettias wilted on the buffet in the breakfast room the first morning of the Crossover Ranch Complete Dispersal Sale when all of the horses but Big Foot were sold. They looked worse the morning the cows were sold. They were dead on the morning of the bull sale.

Before daylight on December 21st, the shortest day of the year, Lovie smashed butter into a blackened waffle she had not rescued from the toaster in time. "Why do you have to sell all the cattle, Mom? You can't run a ranch without cattle. Grampa Hank would use every one of his cusswords at the same time if he knew you were selling off pieces of his ranch to pay taxes—just because he died."

"Why do you think they call it the death tax, Lovie? If Grampa Hank had done a little estate planning, the death tax wouldn't be taking such a huge bite out of the ranch. He didn't even leave a will that I can find. The tax man is the proverbial wolf-at-the-door and the livestock are assets I can sacrifice to keep him from gobbling up the whole ranch. If you're lucky, there'll be a few morsels left for me to pass on to you when you're old enough. Then you'll have to pay estate taxes on the ranch—again!"

"Grampa Hank promised the ranch to me, Mom, not the tax man. Did the tax man ever help him calve, or brand, or wean, or ship or anything else? No way, Jose! And he hasn't been here helping us with these dadgum sales, either, so how come he gets the ranch's assets and I don't? I'm so sore from gathering cattle on Big Foot I can barely sit on my assets."

"That's enough, Lovella! I thought I told you not to ride Big Foot."

"Grampa Hank always let me."

"Grampa Hank is dead."

Lovie jumped to her feet, clanked her orange juice goblet on its crystal coaster and stomped into the kitchen. From a grocery box she was supposed to have already unloaded, she grabbed a granola bar and stuffed it into the pocket of her down vest. She flipped on the light in the mudroom. The glass in the backdoor was covered with frost.

Her coat hung on the mudroom wall beside the hats, slickers and chore coats that Mrs. Grady had not had the heart to give away. Granny and Grampa Hank's boots still stood beneath them. Lovie picked up one of Granny's boots to admire the Crossover Ranch brand stitched into its turquoise top. A sand-colored scorpion lifted its tail when its hiding place was revealed.

"Dadgum!" Lovie ground the scorpion into the tile with her own boot until there was nothing left to pitch out into the pre-dawn darkness. Then she uttered the string of profanities she had inherited from Grampa Hank—so far the only thing she had inherited from Grampa Hank.

"Mary Lovella Grady!" her mother shouted. "If Granny were alive, she'd wash your mouth out with soap and..." Lovie slammed the backdoor and the aroma of early morning coffee followed her into the frigid outside air.

A full moon ducked in and out of dark clouds. Day workers on the cowboy crew were pulling in and parking under the security light by the horse barn. Their horses would soon warn them that the weather was changing for the worse by setting back on halter ropes and banging into trailers as bulky saddles were plunked down on cold backs.

Dingo bounded out of the shadow of the chain-link fenced dumpster yard, nipped at Lovie's heels like a typical Blue Heeler, and dashed ahead to the barn. In the tack room, Lovie turned on the radio for a weather report. The storm had dropped a foot of snow on Santa Fe, giving her dad a legitimate excuse for not joining them at the ranch—his least favorite place on the planet. Unfortunately, from Lovie's perspective, the storm was forecast to stall-out over the Texas Panhandle and would not wreak havoc on the ranch in time to stop the sale.

She clenched her granola bar in her teeth and measured sweet grain into a bucket for Big Foot. The big bay gelding heard her rustling around in the feed room and pawed at the barn door. "Cut it out, Big Foot!" Lovie sputtered through her own mouthful of oats.

Metal screeched against metal as she pushed open the heavy sliding door at the end of the concrete alley. Big Foot flew past her like a big bay bat. Grampa Hank's "old private" arched his muscular neck, shook his head and clattered to his box stall. The handful of saddle horses the day workers had left overnight perked up their ears expectantly. One of them nickered. "Sorry boys," Lovie answered. "You'll just have to wait. Mom's too cheap to buy enough grain for all of you."

Big Foot danced around his grain bucket. No one but Lovie had ridden him since Grampa Hank's accident. She knew it was not Big Foot's fault that he fell over backward and crushed Grampa Hank. Something really awful must have scared him. Big Foot was no outlaw. He was just big—big, powerful and intimidating. He was, therefore, perfect for working the pens and alleys, the job Lovie had chosen today so as not to have to sit near her mother in the sale barn.

Mrs. Grady could not force her daughter to ride poor old broken-down Brownie anymore. Old age had finally claimed him. Brownie had been twenty when Grampa Hank pulled him out of retirement for Lovie. More gray than brown, the wise old gelding quickly learned that he gained nothing by bucking the little girl off. Grampa Hank would just swing her back in the saddle and say, "You're not afraid, are you, Lovella?"

"No, Sir, Grampa Hank," she would respond through tears he pretended not to see. "I'm not afraid of anything. Just don't let go, okay?"

"That's my girl! The only thing to be afraid of is the devil and he's too lazy to get up this early in the morning."

While Big Foot finished eating, Lovie pulled cockleburs out of his long black mane. Every time he heard a strange nicker outside, he jerked his head out of his bucket and slung saliva-coated oats against the barn wall. He switched his long tail and pawed the dirt floor of his stall. Lovie ran her hand under his mane, over the smooth warm part of his neck. "Big Foot, old boy, please just don't make me look stupid in front of the cowboys, okay?" Big Foot backed his ears.

Promptly at 10:00 A.M., as advertised, the Crossover Ranch Complete Dispersal Bull Sale began with everyone in attendance praying that it would be over before the weather deteriorated. By lunchtime, mesquite smoke from the barbecue cookers was blowing into the sale barn each time the doors opened for a new bull to pass through.

Brisket sandwiches, bags of chips and Dr Peppers were passed out to buyers while the sale continued. The sale manager did not want to break the momentum by stopping the sale for lunch. While buyers were fed to keep them in the buying mode, the crew in the pens hustled to keep Grampa Hank's shiny Brangus bulls in front of them.

Lovie's granola bar wore off after the first bull had been pushed from the pens, up the alley, through the sale ring and back to the pens. The thought of a brisket sandwich with onions and pickles and barbecue sauce dripping down her sleeves was beginning to appeal to her—not that she had a free hand to eat with. One held onto Big Foot's long split reins. The other one clutched the saddle horn. Every time the big horse settled down enough to keep the bulls headed in the right direction, the little cowdog nipped him on the heels.

Dingo was overjoyed to be working cattle again. All morning he ran back and forth from bulls' heels to Big Foot's heels, nailing them then ducking as hooves whooshed by his ears. The little tyrant drove bull after bull into the sale ring looking strong and alert—too alert at times. One of Grampa Hank's herd bulls put on a show for the crowd. He blew snot at the man waving the sorting stick and sent him scrambling up and out of the sale ring. A trim woman in leather pants spilled steaming hot coffee all over herself when the man landed in her lap.

Old Cotton, a fluffy white Great Pyrenees, observed Dingo's antics from on top of a stack of hay bales on a flatbed trailer. Three little boys in big hats and bright colored neckerchiefs sat cross-legged at the bottom of the stack, staring up at the giant dog. They ate half their sandwiches then scooted the other halves toward Cotton to encourage her to come down and let them pet her. Lovie nodded to them as she and Big Foot trotted a set of yearlings down the alley.

On the return trip the boys were gone and so was Cotton. Lovie stood up in her stirrups to look for them. A sudden gust of wind set her back down. Instead of a whiff of barbecue brisket, the wind carried a foul odor akin to dead skunk. All at once a man in a dusty, sweat-stained black hat vaulted up the alley fence beside her. Big Foot snorted and planted his feet in the dirt with a tooth-jarring jolt. He swung his powerful hind end into the pipe rails opposite what looked and smelled to him like a predator.

The man's leathery hands held a death grip on the top rail. Semicircles of dirt under his long nails contrasted to his white fingertips. Cotton had treed him up there and the growl rumbling in her chest convinced him to stay put. The wide brim of his hat hid his face as he looked back over his shoulder at the snarling guard dog. He cursed her in Spanish, indifferent to whether Lovie understood him or not—which she did—every word.

A buzzard feather protruded from his snakeskin hatband and the snakeskin toes of his high-heeled boots peeked out over a lower rail—but not much lower. The man was no taller than Lovie. Only his boots were tall. And luckily for him, he had tucked his pant legs into them or Cotton might have already torn them off.

"No, Cotton! No!" Lovie hollered. Dingo crawled out of the alley and slinked away, assuming he was the one being scolded. But Cotton stood her ground with her ruff bristling, never taking her eyes off the man's backside.

His black hat rotated slowly around and his bloodshot eyes peered out from under its brim. The bridge of his nose was wide and flat and an angry red scar marked its center. The disfiguring lump of tobacco in his lower lip was framed by a long, thin black mustache. Tobacco juice leaked out one corner of his sneering mouth and dripped onto the leather vest that molded to his scrawny chest. He seemed reluctant to spit for fear of antagonizing Cotton.

He never spoke. He just glared. Lovie glared back. Big Foot tugged at his bit and rolled its copper cricket with his tongue. Then without being cued, he sidestepped away and lunged at the cloud of dust trailing the last batch of bulls. Lovie felt the man's cold stare following her but she was too busy trying to keep her seat to look back.

Cotton abandoned the stakeout after Lovie and Big Foot were safely away. The old girl sprang back onto the flatbed and scrambled to the top of the bale stack like a youngster. The three little boys did not return.

"Who is that guy with the buzzard feather in his hat?" Lovie asked one of the day workers.

"Nobody you need to know."

"Is that so? Well he stinks. At first I thought maybe a skunk had crawled under the hay trailer and croaked. Is he the tax man?"

"The tax man? Huh...well he'd make a pretty dang good tax man alright. But he ain't."

"What's his name?"

"He calls himself El Lobo."

"I never heard of him. Is he here to buy a bull?"

"Maybe. He got plumb irate when Ms. Grady told the auctioneer to not take his bids."

"Why does my mom care who buys the bulls?"

The cowboy leaned over one side of his horse and pulled up a gate latch. "Mr. Hank caught El Lobo stealin' cattle once. I figure Ms. Grady won't let him have another one even if he pays." He eased his horse through the gate without letting go.

"I can't believe that scumbag has the nerve to show his ugly face here again. I'm gonna go tell him to take a hike!"

"I'd stay away from him if I was you. Every time El Lobo shows up on this outfit there's the devil to pay." He pushed in the gate latch and trotted away with the icy wind biting at the fringe of his chaps.

The crowd attending the bull sale was larger than expected, considering the weather forecast. The P.A. system was cranked up all the way to deafening and the auctioneer's chant reverberated off the corrugated steel walls of the sale barn. The bidding was fierce. The animated ring men hollered, "Yip! Yip!" at the top of their lungs and an astonishing level of excitement was generated by old men buying young bulls.

Mrs. Grady took the auctioneer's microphone at the end of the sale and attempted, in an unsteady voice, to thank everyone for braving the weather to attend. "Your presence is a compliment to my father, Mr. Hank Moore," she managed to say before she choked up.

The auctioneer finished for her. The loudspeaker blared his voice over the back pens where Lovie was. He told the gathering of mostly men, in mostly silver belly hats, that they had been given the opportunity to share the dream of a premier Texas Brangus breeder.

Lovie covered her ears. She was furious that no one seemed to care that when the cattle were all gone, the Crossover Ranch as she knew it would cease to exist. Everyone would leave the sale with a piece of Mr. Hank Moore's dream, except Mary Lovella Grady, his only grandchild.

Lovie led Big Foot back to the horse barn with Dingo following in his footsteps, too tired to nip at his heels. The day workers collected their pay and loaded their horses, as anxious as everyone else to beat a path down the county road before the thickening mist turned to freezing rain. Neighbors did not linger as usual, but picked up chocolate chip cookies and styrofoam cups of hot coffee and headed home to do chores.

Lovie missed the warm camaraderie that used to follow a long cold day of working cattle. She missed the fire burning in the pot-bellied stove in the tack room and the stories swapped while the cowboy crew unsaddled and fed their horses. She missed the pots of Texas chili and plates of buttered cornbread the cook used to spread out on the long table in the cookhouse dining hall. Most of all, she missed the gingerbread Granny always had waiting for her.

"I'd die for another piece of Granny's gingerbread," she sighed, as Big Foot willingly let her unsaddle him. He even let her put her arms around his neck and bury her face in his long mane.

Bull buyers waited their turn at the loading chute, straining to hear winter storm warnings over the rumble of diesel engines. Ranch rigs lined up all the way back to the cattleguard—muddy flatbeds with range cube feeders, shiny duallies lit up like Christmas trees, the usual collection of ¾ ton 4x4s pulling half-top stock trailers, and a new *Chevy Suburban* pulling an aluminum horse trailer with Christmas wrapping sticking out of the saddle compartment.

A loaded cattle truck crossed the creek, looking for a shortcut, and had to turn around at the top of the hill by the old rock chapel. The trucker shuddered at the dark clouds descending on the ranch's namesake—the roughhewn cross over the chapel's bell tower. Lovie wondered if he knew, or cared, that Granny and Grampa Hank were buried nearby in the Crossover Ranch Cemetery. There, marble angels spread their wings over the headstones of four generations of her family...while the Comanchero's unmarked grave sank into the ground outside the fence.

THE ICE STORM

" I can't believe you actually thanked all those men for coming to the bull sale, Mom. I heard one of the ring men say they were just a bunch of old buzzards gathering to pick the meat off a dying ranch."

Mrs. Grady took refuge in Grampa Hank's study. She collapsed into his leather desk chair and turned its high back toward her daughter. "I appreciated their support, Lovie. It's a cinch I'm not getting any from you." With swollen red eyes, still watering from sale-ring sawdust, she squinted at the screen on her laptop. "What time is it, anyway? I have to call our bank in Santa Fe. Hopefully, the bank in Chihuahua released the funds from the volume buyer at the cow sale yesterday. Your dad's worried about the exchange rate. The sooner we get this over with the better for all of us."

"The better for you and Dad, maybe. All you care about is the money. I'm the only one in the family who cares about the ranch. Granny always told me, 'Follow your dreams. Follow your dreams.' It's all she ever talked about. Well the ranch is my dream, Mom. Grampa Hank promised it to me. He promised!"

Mrs. Grady swiveled her chair around, knocking over a stack of books that had been piled by the empty bookcase by the desk. "Believe me, Lovie; I want you to have this place just as much as you do. But since I can't find his will naming you or anybody else as his heir, it makes me his heir by default. I'm his only child, just like you're my only child. The last thing in the world I wanted was to have this ranch dumped in my lap. It might be your dream—but it's my nightmare." She took the crocheted afghan from the arm of the chair and wrapped it around herself. "Your dad will lose some of his orthodontia patients if they find out we have a cattle ranch. Cattle aren't exactly politically correct in Santa Fe, you know. So give me a break. Go pound on Granny's piano or something. My head is already pounding."

The shortest day of the year, was shortened even further by heavy clouds blanketing the Crossover Ranch. The security lights came on early, casting an eerie glow into the dense mist that was freezing to every solid surface. Dormant climbing roses flailed their icy branches against the bay window of the music alcove in Grampa Hank's den where Lovie went to sulk.

She wiped the bottom of a mug of hot chocolate on the sleeve of her sweatshirt and set it down among the family photographs on Granny's grand piano. She did not care if it left a ring. Granny was no longer there to fuss at her for behaving like a cowhand instead of a young lady.

Steam condensed on the picture of Lovie's mother in the fluffy pink prom dress that was still stored somewhere in the main house. The prom queen's tiara sparkled through her golden-blonde curls. Lovie frowned and tipped the picture over on its tarnished silver frame.

Her own hair was flaming red, a curse which seemed to pop up every other generation in her family, beginning with her great-great-grandmother, Lovella-the-first. Lovie felt it was unfair to be cursed by both the hair and the name. She tried to smooth the unruly red corkscrews that kept escaping from her French braid and was glad that a thick layer of dust on the mirror finish of the piano kept her from seeing her reflection.

She took a hymnal from the music stand and ran her fingers over the gold letters of her grandmother's name, June Moore, and made a mental note to add it to the piles of books beneath the empty bookcases on either side of the fireplace. She wondered why the books in every bookcase in the house had been dumped out. She doubted that her father had asked for them for his own library. Grampa Hank's books all had something to do with ranching.

Grampa Hank's treasures filled the den. Oil paintings of ranching scenes and shadow boxes full of arrowheads and rattlesnake rattles lined the plastered rock walls. The fireplace mantle held a collection of kachina dolls from New Mexico. Grampa Hank bought one for Granny every time they visited Santa Fe. Granny would have preferred turquoise jewelry.

Lovie pounded middle C with her thumb. Her spurs jingled across the limestone floor as she felt around for the pedals, but she had no intention of pulling off the boots she had pulled on before daylight. The draft coming from the massive den fireplace made the floor too cold for stocking feet. She longed for the roaring fire Grampa Hank used to stoke in it.

Over the mantle hung the family's heirloom Winchester rifle, guarded by the huge, beady-eyed buffalo head above it. "Hank Moore," Granny used to say. "When are you going to get rid of this buffalo head? It's shedding."

"When hell freezes over," he would answer. "That buffalo was born on this outfit and I'm not kickin' him off just 'cause he's goin' bald.'"

"Hank! Put down your newspaper and look here at your granddaughter. Lovella is introducing her bride doll to your horrible wolf kachina again. She climbs up the bookcases like a little monkey and pulls it off the mantelpiece. Next thing you know, she'll be pulling down that old rifle. To be safe, I'd like to donate it to the county museum. It'd mean a lot to them."

Down came the *Livestock Weekly*. "'That old rifle' means a lot to me, too, Junebug. You wouldn't be standin' here botherin' me if it weren't for 'that old rifle.'"

"Well I don't like to be reminded of the ranch's violent past, Hank."

"I expect you think your great-granny shoulda thrown down her weapon and said, '*Good mornin', Mr. Comanchero. Come inside and slice us a hunk of gingerbread with that Bowie knife you're pointin' at my little Lovella's jugular and we'll chit-chat about ransoms and such.*' No, Ma'm! She bowed up and blasted the thievin' Comanchero skunk right between the eyes and saved her little girl's life—so she could grow up to be your granny and give us this ranch."

Lovie's fingers bore down on the ivories, releasing a cloud of dust from the grand piano's open soundboard. "You promised the ranch to me, Grampa Hank," she said out loud. "You promised. Why did you break your promise?"

Lovie played *Angels We Have Heard on High* from memory because she could not read the music through her tears. Christmas at the ranch would never be the same. Nothing at the ranch would ever be the same. She sent angry glorias ricocheting around the den until her shoulders slumped and her wrists sagged. Her boots slipped off the pedals and the last note faded away.

The wind picked up where the music left off. The fireplace howled like a pack of wolves had been relocated to it. Granny's long lace curtains billowed away from the bay window and a cold draft slid over the back of Lovie's neck. She hunched her shoulders and snapped up the collar of her down vest.

The nametag her mother made her wear to the bull sale was still on her vest pocket. She peeled it off and tried to throw it on the floor but it stuck to her cold fingers. Frozen rain suddenly pelted the window as though it had been aimed at her. She jumped up and the piano bench's claw feet screeched against the floor. She pushed aside a curtain to look outside but all she could see were pellets of ice making glistening trails down the windowpanes.

Lovie's hot chocolate was now cold and covered with scum. She wrinkled her nose at it, exposing the green and red rubber bands on her braces. All of her father's patients wore green and red rubber bands in December. Lovie thought they made her look like she had salad stuck in her teeth twenty-four hours a day. The chattering of her teeth was magnifying the rough places on her braces, but the wax in her vest pocket was too hard to mold over the sharp spots to smooth them out. She headed for the kitchen to soften it in the microwave and make a fresh mug of chocolate.

It was much warmer in the formal living room. Heavy velveteen drapes, protecting the furniture and works of art from sunlight and dust, insulated the room from the storm. Lovie pulled the chain of a stained glass lamp on a marble-topped table. The light bulb flickered and went off. She jiggled the cord but it did not come back on.

She padded across the plush carpet in the dark. Behind her, the lamp flickered on again, creating prisms in the beveled glass doors leading to the main hall. At the other end of the hall, she noticed the light coming from the study. She knew the flickering electricity had not shorted out her mother's laptop or some of the words her mother scolded her for using would be coming from that direction.

She twisted the rheostat on the dining room wall and the chandelier over the mahogany table shone brightly but did not make the room sparkle as it had when Granny was around to dust and polish and fill it with fragrant flowers. Now it smelled like ripe bananas. In the middle of the table was a huge fruit basket, the gift-to-the-boss from the other accountants in Mrs. Grady's accounting firm. The fruit basket and the poinsettias were the only Christmas decorations in the house, other than the green and red rubber bands on Lovie's teeth.

A shuffling sound came from the dark kitchen.

"*Dadgum mice...*" Lovie thought. But the sleet pinging against the windows made it impossible to be sure.

The shuffling came again. "*...lots of dadgum mice.*"

It stood to reason that mice would move into a big, old, unoccupied house. She stomped into the kitchen, making enough racket to scare them away. Something crunched under her boot. The air was filled with the odor of dead skunk. Before she could pull the collar of her vest over her nose, the mudroom door flew open and clanged against the dryer. She dropped the mug she was holding and it shattered at her feet. Enough adrenaline surged through her veins to make her heart beat in her ears. She was suddenly chilled to the bone.

The howling wind shot sleet across the backdoor's open threshold. She lunged at the door to slam it shut then flipped on the overhead light. A startled face appeared in the glass—her own. She pulled down the window shade and twisted the lock in the doorknob. She took a couple of "cleansing breaths," as her mother called them, while her heart rate returned to normal. The wind had also cleansed away the dead skunk smell.

She felt silly locking the door. Granny and Grampa Hank had never locked doors at the ranch. Nobody in the country ever did. When Lovie was little, she could tell if visitors were from the city or country by whether or not they locked their vehicles. City people always locked them. Country people never even took their keys out of the ignition.

Among the pieces of broken mug in the splat of chocolate on the kitchen floor was a crushed buzzard feather. She immediately thought of the buzzard feather on El Lobo's hat. But a buzzard feather could have blown in from anywhere, she told herself. Texas was full of buzzards that feasted on the unfortunate newborn calves that the coyotes tore apart during fall calving. She swept up the mess and dumped it into the trash.

She decided to bring in some firewood and build a roaring fire in the den herself, one of Grampa Hank's "mantle melters." She knew she would not be so jumpy if she could warm up. Then she would sneak Dingo and Cotton inside.

She threw on Grampa Hank's long yellow riding slicker to protect herself from the sleet outside and pulled his old felt hat so low over her ears that it rounded out the crown. She reached for the doorknob to unlock it but could not make herself do it. It was doubtful the worthless caretakers had filled the wood rack in the dumpster yard, anyway, she rationalized. Most likely, there was leftover mesquite on the barbecue trailer in the courtyard...and the dogs were in the courtyard.

Turning on every light that was not already on, she tramped down the main hall. She stopped halfway to stare at the wedding portrait of the first Lovella in the family. Lovie was not afraid of the portrait, but still it seemed to speak to her and she never passed by without stopping to look at it. Lovie looked exactly like her great-great-grandmother, Lovella, the same unruly red hair, the same large eyes and small mouth. Dr. Grady blamed the first Lovella for Lovie's teeth not fitting properly.

According to family lore, however, their appearance was their only similarity. The first Lovella only ventured outside to go light candles in the chapel for the repose of the soul of the dead Comanchero who had taken up residence in her nightmares and refused to leave. The high lace collar of her wedding gown hid the mark made by his Bowie knife when he slashed the cross off her necklace. He was buried with the cross still tightly held in his hand's death grip.

Lovie jumped when she heard a man's voice coming from the study. She continued down the hall and peeked in. Her mother was still wrapped in the crocheted afghan, like a burrito, talking to her father on the speakerphone. The sound of the sleet pouring off the back porch roof masked Lovie's intrusion.

"So you're stormed in and they're stormed out, right, Elizabeth?"

"Right..." Mrs. Grady was preoccupied with rummaging through the top drawer of the desk.

"Speak up, please. I can barely hear you. Are you sure you girls are alright? I've been watching the weather. You're having a full-blown ice storm. Santa Fe got twelve inches of snow and they closed I-25 so I'm snowed-in. Who'll help you load the cattle trucks tomorrow if the crew can't make it back?"

"I cancelled the trucks. The bank in Mexico still hasn't released the funds for the cows and I'm not shipping them out of the country till we get paid."

"But Elizabeth..." Lovie had no desire to listen to another discussion about money but the anxiety in her father's voice made her step into the study. "...what did the sheriff say when you told him El Lobo broke into the house and yanked the books out of all the bookcases? And don't tell me he was just looking for something good to read."

Mrs. Grady quit rummaging and pulled the desk drawer all the way out onto her lap. "He said he can't do anything about it tonight unless it's an emergency. He has his hands full, Honey. The ice storm is snapping the power lines. Our lights have been flickering all evening."

"This is an emergency! Did you tell him El Lobo threatened to get even with your father by stealing our daughter?"

3

EL LOBO

Lovie took a step back and knocked over a bronze statuette on a metal file cabinet. Her mother turned around and gasped at the sight of Grampa Hank's hat and slicker standing before her. The desk drawer in her lap crashed to the floor, spreading its contents all over the study.

"Lovie! Why are you dressed like that?"

"Elizabeth!" demanded the speakerphone. "What's going on? Where's Lovie?"

"I'm here, Dad. I'm wearing Grampa Hank's slicker to go outside for firewood. It's so cold in the den, my wax froze."

Mrs. Grady picked up the receiver and turned off the speaker button. "Sorry, Honey, Lovie startled me. Let me call you back...Okay, I'll tell her...Yes, I promise. Love you. Bye."

"Mom, what did Dad mean about that El Lobo guy getting even with Grampa Hank by stealing me?"

"It doesn't concern you, Lovie. No one but your dad ever took El Lobo's threat seriously. Dad just likes to worry. It makes him feel like he's helping."

"Well, why would the guy trash all the bookcases in the house?" Lovie picked up a book from the floor and flipped through the pages. "Did Grampa Hank stash cash in books?"

"Of course not. If he had, he'd have told me. I was his accountant."

"He didn't tell you where his will was."

Mrs. Grady threw off her afghan, knelt down and began putting pencils, paperclips and business cards back into the drawer. "Lovie, I can't deal with the roller coaster your emotions are on right now. You're angry one minute, your sweet self the next, then angry the next. You're driving me crazy. I understand that anger is one of the stages of grief, especially when people don't get the chance to say goodbye to someone they loved or tell them they're sorry about something or whatever. But you have to find someone else to take it out on." Tears welled up in Mrs. Grady's eyes but she did not cry.

Lovie stood motionless momentarily then she squatted down on the floor beside her mother. "Okay, Mom, I'll try. But can't you please tell me what Dad made you promise to tell me?"

"He wants me to tell you about a tragedy that happened on the ranch involving El Lobo's family. But it really doesn't concern you. You were just a baby."

"Well, I'm not a baby anymore and if a no good cow thief with a bad case of B.O. is threatening to kidnap me because of whatever it is, I think it concerns me, okay?"

Mrs. Grady looked up. "Try harder, Lovie. How did you know El Lobo was a cow thief?"

"One of the day workers told me. Spill your guts, Mom. I'm starting to sweat in this outfit." Lovie took off her hat and unsnapped her slicker. "If you keep a family secret locked in a closet long enough, it turns into a skeleton. I learned that in Health Class. When you're old enough, I'll tell you the other stuff I learned in Health Class."

"Honestly, Lovie."

"Honestly, Mom. I can handle whatever it is you and Dad are keeping secret. Cross my heart and hope to die."

"I'd rather you didn't die. So I'll tell you some of it, but it isn't a subject I intend to dwell on. As I said, it happened when you were a baby. We'd stopped by the ranch to say goodbye to Granny and Grampa Hank after your dad finished his orthodontic residency. We were moving to Santa Fe. Granny was furious that we were leaving Texas."

Lovie opened her mouth to speak but her mother raised her hand. "Let me finish, please. There was a violent thunderstorm that day. After it moved upriver, Grampa Hank rode out to see if the water gaps had washed out. He found some of his cows penned in a hot wire pen below Buzzard Point. You know he never used hot wire down by the river because he was afraid his horses would get tangled up in it. But somebody had. So he hid in the old homestead ruin on the south side of the river to catch whoever came for the cows.

"Pretty soon, here came El Lobo pulling a stock trailer that belonged to the ranch. At the time, he was living in the cookhouse with his wife and little girl. His wife worked for Granny but he pretty much did nothing, so Grampa Hank hired him to ride a few horses. All he ever did, though, was haul his own horse to town to team rope with his buddies.

"Anyway, he stopped the trailer on the north side of the river and unloaded his horse. Grampa Hank could hear that big snorting thing pawing at the water. El Lobo's wife was with him, but I know she wouldn't have been helping him steal if he hadn't made her. She drove the pickup while he rode ahead to guide her over the rock crossing." Mrs. Grady shivered. "The water was up to the running boards by the time they got to the middle of the river and the pickup stalled. El Lobo screamed like a demon and gouged the poor horse with the big old spur rowels he always wore and made him rear up in the headlights. So his wife got out and started to wade back to the riverbank to get away from him. She was carrying their little girl."

Mrs. Grady closed her eyes and took a "cleansing breath." She picked up the afghan beside her and pulled it up to her chin. Lovie noticed that her mother's lips were as blue as the yarn, but she kept quiet.

"Grampa Hank was the first one to hear the wall of floodwater coming down the river. He said he could even smell it. So he fired his varmint rifle in the air to warn them but El Lobo's wife froze in her tracks when she heard the shot. The poor thing was swept away and drowned— so was her little girl—and so was El Lobo's horse. Granny never forgave Grampa Hank for firing that shot. You know how she hated guns."

"That's awful, Mom. But it wasn't Grampa Hank's fault. He tried to warn them. What happened to El Lobo?"

"Absolutely nothing. He managed to get himself out of the river, somehow, and he disappeared. Without any witnesses, Grampa Hank couldn't prove he was trying to steal cattle. We heard by the grapevine that he threatened to get even for the loss of his little girl by stealing you. So your dad was not at all happy to hear that he showed up at the bull sale today. But I wouldn't worry. Now that Grampa Hank is gone, there's no one for El Lobo to get even with."

Mrs. Grady patted Lovie's shoulder and used it to help herself stand up. She picked up the drawer and put it back in the desk. "I don't have a clue what El Lobo was looking for in the bookcases but I'm pretty sure he stole the bracelet your dad gave me for Christmas. I'm positive I put it in this drawer when I was packing my laptop to take to the bull sale. And it's not here now. I haven't told Dad yet. He fusses at me for not locking doors."

Lovie scrambled to her feet. "Oh, no! That rotten thief swiped your new tennis bracelet with all the diamonds? I knew you shouldn't have opened it before Christmas. Dad's gonna freak. This has been a lousy day, huh Mom? As soon as I get the fire going in the den, you can bring your computer in there and warm up. Maybe you'll remember you left it somewhere else."

"Thanks for the invitation. Where's the firewood?"

"There's probably still some on the barbecue trailer in the courtyard."

"Good. I don't want you picking up wood in the thicket tonight."

"Why not? There aren't any more bulls out there, remember?"

Mrs. Grady's face fell. "I'm sorry I had to sell the bulls, Lovie, but believe me; I really had no choice. There are still two truckloads of cows turned out in the Camposanto Pasture by the pens—the ones that were supposed to be shipped to Mexico tomorrow. They're probably bedded down in the thicket and I don't want you spooking them through the courtyard wall. Besides, what if there really is a wolf out there like the caretakers said?"

"Grampa Hank told me there aren't any wolves in this part of Texas." Lovie pulled Grampa Hank's hat down over her ears, snapped up his slicker and stepped out onto the porch.

Icicles were forming on the eves of the metal roofs of all the houses around the courtyard. The uninhabited cookhouse and bunkhouse looked frozen and miserable. Even the cows would have icicles hanging from their winter hair by morning. Their body heat would melt the sleet plastered to their sides by the wind and the bitter cold would refreeze it before it dripped all the way to the ground.

4

THE THICKET

The long back porch of the main house opened to the courtyard. The light pendants hanging from its ceiling were too full of mud dauber nests to shed any light on the dogs' whereabouts. Lovie stepped carefully down the steps to keep from slipping on a thin layer of ice. She stuck her fingers into her mouth to whistle for the dogs but her lips were too cold to cooperate. She fished inside the slicker's pockets for gloves but there were not any.

"Here, Dingo! Here, Cotton!"

She followed the slick stone path to the potting shed in the corner where the barbecue trailer was parked. Dingo got there first. Lovie tripped over him and her bare hands struck the icy stones. The dog licked her nose apologetically.

"Thanks a bunch, Dingo." Dingo wiggled his whole back end and crouched on his bobbed tail. Then he lowered his pointed ears submissively and gave her his less-than-intelligent look. She stroked him under the chin and touched her cold wet nose to his cold wet nose.

Cotton approached from behind and pressed her large body against Lovie's legs. Lovie burrowed her cold fingers into the long, thick hair of the dog's wide shoulders. Dingo gave Cotton a lick on the nose, too, and rolled over on his back, exposing his warm belly.

"Get up, you pitiful thing," Lovie teased. Dingo obeyed for once.

There was no more wood in the wood rack on the barbecue trailer. Lovie checked the wheelbarrow in the potting shed and found none there either. "Dadgum." she said. "What am I gonna to do now?" The dogs sat down beside her to help her figure it out.

Her answer came when the porch lights and the security light near the barn flickered. She knew that if the electricity went off at the headquarters there would be no heat at all in the main house. Glancing back to make sure her mother was not looking out the study window, she pushed the wheelbarrow through the grape arbor that ended at the gate to the Camposanto Pasture.

The forty-acre Camposanto Pasture could not really be considered a pasture on a place as large as the Crossover Ranch where pastures were measured in square miles. It was just a trap or a fenced-in neck of a much larger pasture that went all the way down to the river. It was only used seasonally when cattle were pushed up the creek to the pens or held overnight for early morning shipping. It lay between the headquarters buildings and the chapel and family cemetery on the hill on the other side of the creek. The thicket of mesquites, willows and cottonwoods where the cows where probably bedded down was on the creek.

Lights flickered again, off and on, off and on, making shadows dance on the courtyard wall. Then the electricity went off, and stayed off, and the shadows vanished into the blackness on the other side of the wrought iron gate. Lovie opened it and Dingo shot through in front of the wheelbarrow. Cotton squeezed out too.

"No, dogs!" she hollered. "Dingo, Cotton, get back here! You two can't come. You'll spook the cows for sure." She coaxed them back inside, pushed the wheelbarrow through and shut the gate behind her.

The wind was stronger outside the protection of the walled courtyard. The bare grape vines whipped against the arbor behind her and she could hear the windmill clanking ahead. She was confident she could find the thicket in the dark. She and the dogs had shared many a stick of beef jerky, sitting on the footbridge over the creek in the thicket—hiding from Granny on silver polishing day. She knew that the bulls would have pulverized a few fallen limbs on their way to the pens at the sale barn. While cows tended to pick their way around obstacles in their paths, bulls plowed right through them like the *Dallas Cowboys*.

Lovie used the wheelbarrow like a white cane to find her way around the water tank at the foot of the windmill tower. The mill sounded like it was out of balance and about to fly off into space. At that speed, it should have disengaged automatically. To make matters worse, the float in the tank had iced up and water was spilling over the sides and freezing. The bare ground around it would be a skating rink by morning.

Down the hill a little way, Lovie found the thicket. She filled the wheelbarrow with broken branches and picked up an armload of kindling. The wind prevented her from pinpointing the location of the cows—until a branch snapped sharply on the other side of the thicket. One must have gotten up to stretch and lie back down in a more comfortable spot.

Another branch snapped. The snapping was moving closer. Lovie's arms tightened around her bundle of twigs. She heard the wrought iron gate slam against the rock wall and the dogs came yelping toward the thicket. She caught a whiff of skunk. If the dogs collided with a skunk in the middle of the thicket, the cows would scatter like pool balls and an angry mother and a disobedient daughter would be obliged to gather them in the morning on the ice.

Lovie abandoned the wheelbarrow and ran blindly out of the thicket. She smacked headfirst into the metal leg of the windmill tower, propelling her armload of twigs into the water tank. She bounced backward and sprawled out flat on the frozen ground. Grampa Hank's hat rolled off her head and the dogs trampled it as they scrambled past her. Bright lights flashed somewhere in her head. She hurt too much to move. Before she knew it, the dogs were back, hot on the heels of their prey. All she could do was lie there by the windmill tank, wondering why the skunk smelled dead and hoping, for its sake, that it could either swim or climb.

Dingo seemed determined to break the skunk's eardrums with his high-pitched yapping, while Cotton snarled viciously. It was a frightening sound, even to Lovie, who could only moan. Dingo returned to her prone body and licked her eyelids and her nose and mouth.

Then the lights in her head went out.

Thunder rumbled, long and low. Lovie's whole body felt the vibration, as though it were coming from underground rather than from the sky. It was almost comforting, like being asleep in her mother's *Land Rover* on the long trip to the ranch. Instead of sleet stinging her face, she had the sensation of raindrops gently patting her eyelids. But she began to feel nauseous and managed to roll over on her stomach. She wanted to lie there and let the raindrops pit-a-pat the back of her slicker but her French braid was channeling cold water down her back. Her head began to pound and every breath she took smelled like skunk.

She scooched to her hands and knees, crawled to the water tank and pulled herself up. Surprisingly, her wet hands did not freeze to the tank's metal rim. Rain had washed away all the ice. She could not hear the dogs barking anymore. Instead, she heard the unmistakable beller of a bull. Before she could wonder how a bull escaped the bull sale, lightning struck the thicket.

The searing sound was simultaneous with an earth shattering thunder boom and the split second of light revealed El Lobo climbing down the windmill tower above her. El Lobo was the skunk the dogs had been after.

Lovie lunged for the courtyard wall, trying not to slip in the mud—soft mud that should have been frozen hard. "Dingo! Cotton! Come!" she commanded. But no dogs came. Her hands scraped against the wet rocks of the wall but it was too high and too slippery to climb over so she ran alongside, hunting desperately for the gate. She fell to her knees when her arms plunged through its wrought iron scrollwork.

The main house was still dark, but the cookhouse and the bunkhouse had sprung to life. "Mom! Help me! Mo-o-om!" Lovie screamed. Her head felt like it would explode. She swung into the courtyard and did not pause to close the gate behind her.

She raced through the grape arbor through vines that slapped her face with wet green leaves. She did not stop to wonder why there were still some green leaves on the dormant vines. Like a big yellow bird, she flew across the courtyard toward the cookhouse, past the fountain with the life-size marble angel in the middle. Grampa Hank's long slicker snagged a nearby rose bush and rose petals filled the air. The bush was chock-full of succulent white roses; roses that were red last summer—roses on thorny canes that had been frozen stiff only minutes before.

"Mo-o-o-om!"

Lovie cleared the steps to the cookhouse porch in one giant leap and left muddy skid marks all the way to the entryway door. It opened before she touched it. Her boots skidded out from under her on the gleaming wood floor and she fell flat on her back for the second time tonight. She gasped for air and stared wide-eyed at the bottoms of the chaps and jackets hanging on the entryway wall. The air smelled like gingerbread.

The bulbs of the deer antler chandeliers in the long dining hall hurt her eyes. She shielded them with her dirty hands then slowly spread her fingers apart. A pair of turquoise-topped boots stood inches from her nose. A woman's legs held them up. But they were not her mother's legs. A liver-spotted hand reached down to help her. Among the large turquoise rings on the bony fingers, was Granny's platinum wedding band.

"Granny?"

5

THE COOKHOUSE

Granny withdrew her hand when Lovie did not respond. "Lovella? What in heaven's name are you doing here?"

Lovie's mouth fell open as though she expected *M&M*s to drop into it. "Granny, is that you? Am I...dead, too?"

Granny squinted. "You don't look dead."

"Neither do you. I must be dreaming then." Lovie squeezed her eyes closed. "Good night, Granny."

"Of course you're dreaming, Lovella. You're dreaming that you're a doorstop. Now, move over. I need to close the door. I can see by your mop of wet hair that you know very well it's raining outside."

The cowbells hanging from the doorknob jangled as the entryway door closed.

"Dadgum...my head really hurts. Dreams aren't supposed to be painful, are they, Granny?"

"How many times do I have to tell you that dreams are only painful when you don't have them? Without your dreams to follow, you'll fall into the bottomless pit of hopelessness."

"Now I know I'm dead. And I'm being punished by having to listen to your 'Follow Your Dreams' speech again."

Granny leaned over and thumped her granddaughter on the ear. "Get up off the floor, Lovella. You're soaking wet."

Lovie sat up and laughed. She shook off the pounding in her head and hugged her grandmother's legs. "It really is you, isn't it? I thought I'd never see you again. Why are you so cold? Where is Grampa Hank? He needs to build you a fire."

Granny struggled to keep her balance. "We don't build fires in June.

Is that Grampa Hank's slicker you're wearing? Is he responsible for your unexpected visit?"

Lovie let go of Granny's legs. "My unexpected visit? What about your unexpected visit?"

"I don't have to visit my own ranch, Lovella. Is your mother with you? Or did she just drop you off and leave like she usually does."

"She's in Grampa Hank's study working on the books from the bull sale."

"What bull sale? Your Grampa Hank doesn't sell bulls in June."

Lovie stood up slowly. "Why do you keep saying June? It's December. It's nearly Christmas. Aren't you happy to see me?"

"Quit babbling, Lovella. I know perfectly well when June is. I was born in June. My name is June and I...never mind. What I don't know is how you've dropped in unannounced. I should be informed of the comings and goings at the Crossover." Granny lifted Lovie's chin with cold fingers. "You've grown, haven't you? And you're getting your teeth straightened. Perhaps now you could make yourself useful in the house, like a young lady, instead of gallivanting about the ranch with the cowhands all day."

"But Granny..."

"But nothing. I have a list of things to accomplish and I can't afford any disruptions. Scoot on out to the greenhouse and bring me another wheelbarrow of long stemmed bluebonnets. And don't wheel them across this clean floor. Park them in the breezeway. We'll be arranging them in the kitchen."

"But the ranch doesn't have a greenhouse."

"Don't dispute my word, Lovella. I always dreamed of having greenhouses and now I have three of them. Why are you sweating? What do you have on underneath that slicker—a down vest? You must be burning up. No wonder you're acting so strangely."

Granny put a cold hand on Lovie's forehead. "You are burning up! If you're sick, your mother should be here taking care of you, not me. I have my own work to do."

The timer in the kitchen buzzed. "I'll have Maria bring you some gingerbread," Granny said as she went to go see about it. "Gingerbread makes everyone feel better."

A bead of sweat ran down Lovie's face as Granny disappeared through the swinging kitchen door. She brushed it away along with a tear. "Why aren't you as happy to see me as I am to see you, Granny?"

Lovie took off her slicker and vest. For the first time in her existence, the smell of gingerbread was making her nauseous but the dining hall floor was way too clean to throw up on. Earlier this afternoon, the floor had been filthy. Bull buyers had tracked in dirt and manure while looking for sale catalogues; while looking for the coffee pot; while looking for the bathrooms. Now everything sparkled.

"I'm way past sick," Lovie thought. *"I'm hallucinating."*

She went unsteadily to the window seat by the fireplace and slumped into the cushions. Rather than a roaring fire, the fireplace was filled with buckets of fresh bluebonnets. She had never seen bluebonnets with stems so long. She had never seen bluebonnets that were not blue. The buckets contained blue ones and pink ones both.

She cupped her hands around her eyes and pressed them against the window. The rain had slowed to a trickle. The trees in the courtyard were all leafed out and their trunks and branches twinkled with tiny white lights instead of ice crystals. But the main house remained dark.

The kitchen door swung open and a plump woman burst into the dining hall. Lovie could not help but notice the ornate gold-filigree cross she was wearing. It had a large red stone in the middle and stood out against the starched white bib of the apron flaping around the legs of her faded blue jeans. She made a beeline for Lovie, flailing one arm wildly. "Mary Lovella! Look at you. You are all grown up. Is your mother with you?"

Lovie tensed to flee from the window seat, but the woman's smiling face was in her own before she could escape. With one last shake of the wrist, the woman pointed a thick glass thermometer in the direction of Lovie's mouth.

"I'm sorry this is necessary, *m'ija*, but your Granny wants me to take your temperature."

"Hey wait a minute! That's a calf thermometer." Lovie pushed it away and clamped her hands over her mouth.

"*Calmate, m'ija.* Calm yourself. I soaked this one in alcohol. It is safe. I boiled the last one but it exploded. Please open your mouth."

"No way."

The woman looked hurt. "*Pobrecita,* poor thing. You are afraid of me, no?"

"No. I'm not afraid of anything. Who are you?"

"My name is Maria. I am the cook for your Granny's ranch. See?" Maria proudly spread the skirt of her apron to show the Crossover Ranch brand embroidered on the pocket. "Your mother has told you about me, no?"

"No. Does my mom know you?"

"Oh yes, *m'ija.*"

Lovie resigned herself to having her temperature taken. She examined the cook's animated face, framed by short salt and pepper hair. It was obvious that the wrinkles around her full mouth and large brown eyes came from smiling. "Your cross is beautiful, Maria," she said with the thermometer clamped in her teeth.

"Thank you. My husband gave it to me for a wedding present. It was the only thing he had of value. But he is no longer with us. Please do not talk with the thermometer in your mouth. Every time you do, you must keep it there three minutes more."

Maria smoothed back the ringlets of red hair that were sticking to Lovie's forehead. "You have a very large bump here, Mary Lovella." Maria pressed it with her thumb.

"Ouch!" Maria's thumb was ice cold. Lovie turned away and hid in her thoughts while the thermometer registered a temperature. *"Maybe I froze to death...I said I'd die for another piece of Granny's gingerbread, but I didn't mean it literally...Maybe I got trampled to death...I heard a bull in the thicket, but I thought Mom sold all the bulls...Maybe I got struck by lightning."*

Lovie spit out the thermometer. "Lightning! I saw El Lobo when the lightning struck! I have to find Mom. I have to tell her El Lobo is in the Camposanto Pasture."

Maria's face turned the color of her apron. She grabbed onto her cross with both hands. *"Madre de Dios.* Are you sure it was El Lobo?"

"Yes! The lightning struck and I saw him climbing down the windmill so I ran back to the courtyard. The lights were off in the main house so I came here. I thought Mom was here but it was Granny."

Maria made the sign of the cross. "Excuse me, please," she whispered and scurried into the kitchen with her apron flapping.

While the swinging door was still swinging, Lovie got up and tiptoed to the entryway door. The mother whose company she had been avoiding for weeks was suddenly the only person she wanted to be near. The cowbells jingled and jangled as she tried, without success, to budge the rain-swollen door from its tight wooden frame.

6

GRANNY

Lovie felt a cold hand on her shoulder.

"Wait, Lovella," Granny opened the entryway door with ease. "We won't bother with the bluebonnets tonight. I'm taking you to the house. You've upset Maria."

"Fine with me. I have to talk to Mom."

"Why would your mother be sitting over there in the dark?"

"Because your electricity went off."

Light poured from the windows of the cookhouse and bunkhouse behind them and twinkled all around the courtyard. The main house was the only unlit residence. The air outside was heavy with the scent of roses. Lovie picked a fragrant white one from a cane climbing up a porch post.

Granny snatched it out of her hand. "Look here, Lovella. It was cruel of you to mention El Lobo in front of Maria. She is terrified of him. El Lobo is evil."

"But I saw him, Granny. He's following me."

"What have you done to make evil follow you?"

"Nothing."

"Well you must have done something. Think about it. Is there anything you need to apologize for?"

"Okay, how's this. I'm sorry a stinking freak is trying to kidnap me. But it's not my fault. It's because of what Grampa Hank did—what you never forgave him for."

"That's no concern of yours."

"Why does everybody keep telling me that? Whose concern is it?"

"No one's—unless he follows you here. No one is allowed on my ranch without an invitation. By the way, who invited you?"

"Since when do I need an invitation?"

Lovie followed Granny across the botanical garden that had sprung up in the courtyard. White blossoms covered all the shrubs and mounds of white flowers erupted from planters and flowerbeds. The flower mounds seemed to glow.

Granny paused beside a wooden gazebo under construction. Stepping over bundles of wet lumber, she inspected each of the six columns holding up the hexagonal roof and seemed pleased.

"Granny, this is the gazebo from the plans Mom and I found under your bed, isn't it?"

"I'll thank the two of you to stay out from under my bed, Lovella. I've waited a long time for this gazebo and my carpenters have promised to have it completed before the wedding this weekend. Grampa Hank couldn't tear himself away from his other wives long enough to build it himself."

"Dadgum. Grampa Hank has other wives?"

"His cows, Lovella. The man is married to his cows. Thank goodness Pete knows there's more to a ranch than just a herd of cattle."

"Who's Pete?"

"Pete is my graduate student. He's doing research for his master's thesis, 'Maximizing Ranch Resources through Alternative Enterprises.' He'll be getting married in our chapel on Saturday."

The sound of a woman's screams pierced the night. Lovie grabbed Granny's sleeve. "Who's that?"

Granny pulled her arm away. "It's only peacocks. I didn't like them at first but they do make good watch birds. And they're quite beautiful. They roost in the thicket, but they're not allowed in the courtyard so be sure to leave the gate closed."

Lovie wondered how a closed gate would keep out a bird that could fly up a tree to roost. She hurried over to close the gate she had left open earlier, not wanting to think about what these new watch birds might be watching. She caught up with Granny as she was unlocking the door to the main house.

Granny flipped on the hall light. "You were wrong, Lovella. The electricity did not go out. Now take off those filthy boots and spurs and go hang your things in the mudroom. When will you ever start acting like a young lady?"

Lovie sat down on a hooked rug at the bottom of the stairs and struggled to remove the boots that were now like a second layer of skin. "When did you start locking the house and keeping watch birds?"

Granny answered over her shoulder as she climbed the stairs. "To keep someone from walking off with my night bloomers."

"Your what?"

"I have genetically engineered flowers for nighttime weddings. The blooms glow in the dark. I keep the seeds locked in the vault."

"I didn't know you had a vault."

"Well, I do. I'm going to bed now. I have a lot to do before the wedding. You can sleep in your mother's room. I assume whoever invited you here will come for you in the morning."

"I hope it was Grampa Hank. Where is he?"

"He's at the River Camp. He has talked Pete to helping him brand the late calves and spray the cows for horn flies. I'm quite sure he will not be coming to the headquarters tomorrow." Granny ducked into her bedroom at the top of the stairs.

Lovie peeked into the study to look for signs of her mother's accounting activities, but there were none. All the books were back in the bookcase. The laptop was gone. There were no dog-eared ledger sheets or stacks of registration papers anywhere in sight. The desk calendar read, June 21st. She turned it to December 21st and picked up the phone. There was no dial tone.

Upstairs, Lovie found Granny standing by her dressing table, taking off her turquoise jewelry.

"Why are you so dressed up, Granny?"

"I'm not dressed up. I'm dressed properly. This is how I dress to receive my guests, although we won't be having any guests this week because of the wedding."

"How can you have a wedding without guests?"

"I'm not talking about wedding guests. I'm talking about paying guests."

"Dadgum. You're not turning the place into a dude ranch, are you?"

"Heavens no. I don't want to attract any more would-be cowhands than we already have. I don't want any hunters either, especially bird hunters. They're always losing their dogs. Dogs are as much of a nuisance as cows. My paying guests are all bird watchers, quiet refined birders. And if the wedding on Saturday is as lovely as I expect it to be,

I'll run ads for wedding packages in birding magazines."

Lovie burst out laughing. "Grampa Hank is letting you take in bird-watching lovebirds? The price of beef must be really rotten."

"It is immaterial to me whether you or your grandfather approve of the way I manage this ranch now. It is my ranch. My grandmother gave it to me and it is my turn to run it the way I please. Grampa Hank had his turn. I happen to know that it brings urban people pleasure to be able to spend weekends in this lovely old home with thousands of acres on which to hike and picnic and watch for unusual birds."

Lovie giggled all the way down the hall, thinking her grandmother had turned into an unusual bird herself. But the giggles stopped when she stepped into her mother's bedroom. The bed was all made up. The needlepoint pillows that her mother always tossed onto the floor were lined up against the headboard. There were no suitcases flung open and covered with her mother's unfolded clothes, no limp jogging clothes hanging from the bedposts or socks sticking out from under the bed ruffles. All the newspapers and half-drunk cups of coffee that surrounded her mother were nowhere to be seen.

She turned on the light over her mother's wedding portrait and sat down slowly on the bed to gaze at the only thing she seemed to have left of her mother. The young bride's pretty face was framed by a lace mantilla. The mantilla was long, falling to rest on yards upon yards of creamy satin. The gown was the most beautiful dress Lovie had ever seen. In her mind, the main reason for marriage was the promise of wearing it someday.

Granny stepped into the bedroom, wearing a long white bathrobe. Her braided bun was unpinned and her thin silver hair hung in crimped waves past her shoulders. She had cold cream on her face.

"You might not be a ghost, Granny, but you sure look like one."

Granny was looking at the portrait. "Having another wedding at the ranch is a dream come true for me. Your mother's wedding was glorious. We barbecued and baked for days. We didn't bake a big, extravagant wedding cake, though, like they do now. The tradition in the country was for all the neighbors to bring small ones. They were decorated in every shade of pink imaginable."

Lovie had her mother's wedding story memorized but she knew better than to stop her grandmother from telling it again.

"Grampa Hank smiled big enough to show his missing teeth and told everyone how proud he was to be getting an orthodontist in the family. He was polite to his new son-in-law, even though he thought the boy was rather strange."

"Dad isn't strange—for an orthodontist. Lots of people are afraid of large animals."

"He's afraid of dogs, too."

"Just Cotton. Cotton is a large animal. Can we open the windows, Granny? I can't breathe in here." Lovie peeled off the maroon *Texas Aggie* sweatshirt she had on over her t-shirt.

"Where did you get that hideous t-shirt, Lovella?"

Lovie looked down at her faded black shirt which sported the ghostly white face of a space alien with huge green eyes and a tiny round mouth. "Dad bought it for me in Roswell at the UFO Museum. It glows in the dark just like your flowers. He said it reminded him of me. Okay—he's a little strange—but in a good way."

"It broke my heart when your father decided to open his practice in Santa Fe. I begged your mother not to leave Texas. It was her duty to carry on the legacy of this ranch that has been in our family for so many generations."

"What about me?"

"What about you, Lovella? You've turned into a ruffian just like your grandfather."

"I have not. Just because I'm not afraid of cattle and horses and dogs doesn't make me a ruffian. I know how to play the piano like you taught me. And Mom taught me how to set the table in the dining room with her china and silver and crystal."

"I'm surprised. Your mother told me she never put anything on the table that couldn't go in the dishwasher, the microwave or the trash can. Angela is the only girl I've found who really appreciates the fine heirlooms in this house. She even enjoys helping me polish silver. In that regard, she is more of a daughter to me than your mother."

"What a rotten thing to say about Mom. No wonder she doesn't want the ranch. Who are you and what have you done with my Granny?" Lovie pulled her alien shirt over her face so that the alien gaped at Granny. "Who's Angela, anyway?" the alien mouthed. "Nobody on earth likes to polish silver—or on Mars either."

"Angela is Pete's fiancée. Good night, Lovella. There's a clean nightgown in the bottom drawer of the dresser."

The bedroom was stuffy. The upstairs bedrooms were always stuffy in the summertime. Lovie opened the dormer window. She remembered sitting on the window seat when she was little, watching the cardinals come and go from the angel statue in the middle of the fountain. She heard someone talking and saw a young couple sitting on the fountain's edge, holding hands. She closed her eyes and turned away.

Her head still hurt. "*If this is a dream, it's Granny's dream, not mine,*" she thought. "*At least El Lobo isn't allowed in. How did I wind up getting stuck in it?*" In the drawer, she found a pink cotton nightgown trimmed in Battenberg lace and questioned the sanity of lace on a garment that was meant to be worn in the dark. An oversized t-shirt would have been more comfortable. She looked for a toothbrush but couldn't find one. "*Oh well. If I'm already dead, tooth decay can't kill me.*"

She turned off the light over her mother's wedding portrait. "*One of us is lost, Mom. Is it you or is it me?*"

7

MARIA

Lovie turned her aching head from side to side and struggled to wake up. She heard Dingo barking and felt him trying to pry her eyelids open with his warm slimy tongue. She tried to push him away but he just yapped louder and licked harder.

Then all was quiet.

She raised her head from the feather pillow. As usual, her damp hair was stuck to the sides of her face. Her head still ached but not as much as it had the night before. She reached back and touched the bedstead's polished headboard and probed the footboard with her bare feet. She was still in her mother's bed and there were no dogs in bed with her. The clock on the bedside table read 5:02 A.M. She squinted at it again. THURSDAY—JUNE 22. She knocked it off the bedside table and buried her face in the pillow.

The damp, early morning air flowing through the open window made her shiver. She felt around for the covers that had slipped onto the floor, then climbed out of bed to pick them up and close the window. The glowing flower mounds in the courtyard had more blossoms than they had the night before. They were beginning to cascade over the sides of the planters.

"Granny's flowers are weird." she whispered to herself. "Poor Grampa Hank."

She dressed in the same dirty clothes she had worn the day before and pulled on the same dirty socks. She undid her tangled French braid and tied her hair back with a maroon scrunchie she found in her jeans' pocket along with an ear tag marker from the bull sale. Then she tiptoed down the hall to go downstairs and take another look at Grampa Hank's study.

Granny's bedroom door was closed, but Lovie did not knock. Grampa Hank never woke Granny before daylight without a cup of coffee in his hand. From the landing, she could smell coffee brewing downstairs. It reminded her of her mother. She leaned over the banister and called, "Mom, are you down there?" With no one around to catch her, she threw her leg over the banister and slid down—a little too fast. The hat rack by the newel post crashed onto the wood floor. She glanced back at Granny's closed door before setting it upright.

"Good morning, Mary Lovella!" Maria breezed down the main hall wearing a fresh white apron. Her gold cross caught Lovie's eye again. It was hard to miss with what appeared to be a sizeable oval ruby set in the middle. Maria flashed Lovie a smile and handed her a steaming mug of frothy hot chocolate complete with marshmallows.

"Thanks, Maria." Lovie followed Maria to the kitchen, licking marshmallow off her upper lip. "Is my mother here?"

"No, m'ija. I am sorry. I fixed a plate of gingerbread for you. You did not eat any last night. Would you like it now?"

"No thank you." Between the ache in her head and the ache in her heart at the thought of her mother being left alone with El Lobo, she felt queasy. But she decided not to mention him to Maria again. "Is Granny awake?"

"Oh, yes. She rode to the River Camp with the branding crew to ask Mr. Hank for a load of manure for the greenhouses. It makes very good fertilizer after Pete sterilizes it with solar power."

"What a guy. He leaves it out in the sun till it doesn't stink anymore, right? Did you say Granny rode...horseback?"

"Oh, no, m'ija. No one went horseback. Mr. Hank keeps the horses at the River Camp, all except for the one he left here at the barn for you. I will go there soon to prepare the noon meal."

"Then why didn't someone wake me up? I really want to talk to Grampa Hank and he won't want to talk to me if I'm late to a cattle working. It'll take me an hour to saddle and ride all that way now. When are you going, Maria? Maybe I can still get there in time to help them vaccinate the calves."

"I am sorry, but you cannot go with me. Your Granny said for you to stay here and help bake wedding cookies with Angela."

"But I want to help Grampa Hank. I've vaccinated calves with him ever since he showed me the difference between intramuscular and subcutaneous. Who'll number the ear tags? Mine never fade, ever. Look, I still have an ear tag marker in my pocket from yesterday. I don't want to stay home and bake cookies with some girl I don't even know." Lovie retrieved her boots from the mudroom. "I want to go help Grampa Hank!"

Maria reached out to smooth Lovie's kinky hair. "Mr. Hank does not need your help today, *m'ija*. He has Pete."

An enormous orange cat wrapped its fluffy tail around Lovie's knees and revved up its purr.

"Fireball? I thought the coyotes ate you. You better not let Grampa Hank catch you in the house, kitty-cat." She scooped him up and stroked his long orange fur. "You're all wet. Were the dogs chasing you last night?"

"The headquarters has no dogs, Mary Lovella. Your Granny does not allow dogs near her flowers."

"But Grampa Hank loves dogs. He hates cats. He thinks cats are more destructive than mice. He only let me keep Fireball at the ranch one summer because I promised to take him home, but the coyotes ate him... at least I thought the coyotes ate him."

Maria poured herself some coffee and added cream until it was nearly white. She poured the remaining cream into a saucer and set it down on the mudroom floor. "Fireball has to stay in the house so he will not bother the scissortails. Bird watchers love scissortails. They love all of the birds here."

"Even the ones that scream at them at night?"

Maria's smile lines deepened. "The peacocks are Pete's. They were free with a shipment of guineas he ordered to eat the grasshoppers but..."

"Let me guess. The coyotes ate the guineas."

"Most of them. Yesterday's rain will get rid of the grasshoppers, though, and Pete predicts that the sun will shine on the branding. I do not like to leave Angela alone when it is raining. She is like a Border Collie when it thunders—very high strung."

"Why is Grampa Hank working the cattle on the other side of the river? The pens at the River Camp are sorry. I'm surprised he keeps the saddle horses there."

"All of the cattle except a few yearling bulls are on that side. The bird watchers do not like cattle. They cannot understand that the mama cows do not want them to pet their calves so your Granny asked Mr. Hank to move them."

"And he did it? The pastures there aren't big enough for all his cattle. They'll stomp out all the grass. I don't understand why Grampa Hank is letting Granny make all these goofy changes. Please tell him I need to talk to him as soon as he comes back."

"He is not coming back. He is helping Pete rebuild the old homestead ruin at Buzzard Point so Pete and Angela will have a nice place to live after the wedding. It is a surprise for Angela. Your grandparents are very generous, you know. They love Angela like a daughter, Mary Lovella."

Lovie frowned. "I hope she likes buzzards flying over her honeymoon cottage. Why do you keep calling me, Mary Lovella, anyway? The only time my mother calls me that is when she's mad at me."

"I am sorry, *m'ija*, but I have always called you that."

"Always? Last night was the first time you ever laid eyes on me."

"Oh, no. I was there when you were born. You were named after me."

"I'm sorry, but my name is Mary Lovella, after my great-great grandmother, Lovella."

"And Mary, after me—Maria—Maria Elena Guadalupe Rios Lopez."

"Whatever. Where is this girl I'm supposed to be baking cookies with?"

"In the cookhouse, polishing silver."

"She's polishing silver this early in the morning? Pete's fiancée is as weird as he is. Who is she anyway?"

Maria straightened her apron and smiled sweetly. "Angela is my daughter."

Fireball sauntered back to Lovie, licking cream off his whiskers. He stood up and pressed his front paws against her leg to stretch and poked his sharp claws through her jeans. Over Maria's protest, Lovie tossed him outside to torment the birds. A spot of blood appeared on her pant leg. She was relieved to see that it was still red.

8

ANGELA

Fireball lumbered ahead of Lovie as she dragged herself to the cookhouse for her prearranged meeting with Angela. The tip of the cat's fluffy orange tail twitched as he trotted.

"What are you so excited about you big glutton? You're looking for another saucer of cream, aren't you?"

They made their way around the fountain where the young couple had been holding hands the night before. The marble angel seemed to watch them as they passed. The angel was a gift to the first Lovella from her husband, to coax her outside into the sunshine more. But the poor thing never recovered from her encounter with the Comanchero. Now, the fountain was just a place for dead leaves to float on stagnant rainwater. Its pipes were corroded and Grampa Hank refused to replace them because he did not believe in "wastin' water on goldfish." The water used to pour from the statue's upraised palms but now its palms were dry and cracked.

Fireball attacked the end of a peacock's tail as it hung limply out of one of the planters. The big bird lifted its crested head momentarily then plunged it back into the bounty of white blossoms. His iridescent blue neck was a blur as he harvested the flowers as fast as he could.

"Hey, you! Get out of there!" Lovie waved her arms and the peacock hopped onto the courtyard wall and sailed to the drinking tub on the other side. Twisted vines of glow-in-the-dark flowers had spread all around the tub and were climbing the legs of the windmill tower.

The peacock found a peahen pecking its way around the tub and displayed his brilliant spotted tail for her. She ignored him so he went back to plucking white blossoms off the prolific vines.

Fireball was waiting in the breezeway between the cookhouse and the bunkhouse, twitching his tail irritably. Lovie opened the kitchen door and the cat darted in.

A slender girl in a fuzzy pink bathrobe and rubber gloves took one look at Fireball and vaulted into the nearest kitchen chair. She held a large silver tray to her chest, like a shield. "Get him out of here, Lovie!" she squealed. "He has a mouse!"

The girl shifted her weight from one bare foot to the other, aware that the only thing protecting her toes was pink nail polish. Her dark eyes were wide with fright and they grew wider when Fireball hid under her chair. "Quick! Throw him out before he lets it go!"

Lovie was in no mood to take orders. "Hi. You must be Angela."

"Yes, I'm Angela. Please, Lovie, please throw Fireball outside. He's going to drop the mouse."

Angela was older than Lovie, thinner, and standing on the chair she seemed much taller. Her sleek waist-length hair was so black that it had blue highlights. Lovie thought she looked like the model at her mother's favorite boutique in Santa Fe, with high cheekbones and a flawless complexion that was unmarked by the freckles that dotted her own face.

"Mice won't hurt you unless they eat the cheese off your cheeseburger." Lovie knelt down on the floor and dragged Fireball out from under the chair by his tail, taking care not to dislodge the creature hanging out of his mouth.

Then, with a gasp, she turned loose of the cat and crawled behind Angela's chair. "Angela, it's not a mouse. It's a bat!"

Fireball turned loose of the bat and watched it flop helplessly on the polished linoleum. He nudged it with his paw and the creature took to the air, flying erratically around and around the girls, barely missing them on each fly-by. Lovie threw her arms around the chair, entrapping Angela's cold bare feet.

"What are we supposed to do now?" Lovie asked.

Angela began to giggle, ducking and dodging to avoid the bat. "We? You're the one who turned a bat loose in the kitchen."

"How can you be afraid of mice and not bats?" Lovie demanded.

"Pete says bats won't hurt you unless they have rabies."

"How am I supposed to know if the dadgum thing has rabies? For all I know it's a vampire bat. What if it sucks out our blood and gives us rabies too?"

"Don't be silly. Pete is doing research on the bats at the ranch. He says we don't have any bloodsucking bats, only the kind that eat flying insects."

"We don't need bats to eat flying insects. There's a can of bug spray under the sink."

"Pete says bug spray is bad for the environment. He says every creature has a function in the ecosystem, even centipedes and stinging scorpions. Now let go of me so I can go open the door and let the bat out."

The bat made a few more passes around the kitchen then escaped to find a safer place to hang around. Fireball lunged at it and missed.

"Pete is really smart, Lovie. He's good with his hands too. Did you notice the fountain? Pete is going to fix it for Granny to thank her for letting us get married in her chapel. And he's going to raise guppies in it and drop them in all the puddles around the ranch to eat mosquito larva to help the bats keep the mosquitoes down. He helps Granny with her flowers and birds, too. You don't mind if I call her, Granny, do you? She's like a grandmother to me too."

Lovie did mind. "How old are you, Angela? You don't look old enough to get married."

"I'm nineteen. Mama got married when she was seventeen."

"Wow. How old was your dad?"

"I don't know. I haven't seen Papa since I was a little girl."

If Lovie had not been feeling so sorry for herself, she might have felt sorrier for Angela. It hurt her that Grampa Hank did not need her help, perhaps did not even want her help. But Angela did. And since it was obvious that Grampa Hank would not be answering any of her questions this morning, Lovie decided she might as well help Angela bake the *biscochitos* for her wedding. *Biscochitos* were Lovie's favorite cookie, a treat that traditionally came with Christmas in Santa Fe.

When the last of the dozens and dozens of *biscochitos* was rolled in cinnamon-sugar and the mess was cleaned up, Angela announced that it was time to make the rolls for the rehearsal dinner. Lovie watched impatiently as Angela threw together two huge bowls of yeasty dough and covered them with damp dishtowels to rise. Then for a little extra fun—in Angela's opinion—they made a quadruple recipe of chocolate chip cookie dough with extra chocolate chips "just for Pete."

Angela gave Lovie a cold hug when the job was finally done and handed her a spoonful of cookie dough. "Mama said you weren't feeling well last night. This will cure you. But if you eat too much raw dough, you will get worms."

"I hope you know that's an old wives' tale, Angela. But, if I do get worms, my guess is that your fiancé, Pete, will think up something for me to swallow to get rid of them. Why don't I take these two cookie sheets to the main house and bake them in Granny's oven? We'll get done a lot faster that way."

Lovie breathed a sigh of relief as she joined Fireball in the fresh air of the courtyard. She could not remember ever spending so much time in a kitchen. The courtyard was Fireball's idea of heaven. The humidity from last night's rain and the stillness of the morning magnified the squawking of the birds. The sun shone golden on the chapel at the top of the hill, but Lovie noticed an ominous blue-gray line of clouds hugging the horizon behind it. Pete had assured Maria that the sun would shine on the branding. If so, it was looking like it had better be a very short branding.

9

THE VAULT

Lovie rocked Fireball in the swing on the back porch of the main house and waited for the cookies to bake. The cat's bulky body slopped over both sides of Lovie's lap. He was not warming her legs as she had hoped. He was only putting them to sleep.

Angela came out of the cookhouse and flounced gracefully across the patio. She had changed into culottes and a crisp white blouse and was waving a manila envelope. Her radiant expression turned gloomy when she noticed the darkening line of clouds behind the chapel.

"Hey, Angela," Lovie called to her. "Have you seen the peacocks eating the blooms off Granny's glow-in-the-dark flowers?"

"The only one that eats them is the biggest one with the longest tail. Chase him away whenever you catch him. Granny worked so hard in the greenhouses growing the seeds that it's sad to let him eat all the pretty flowers."

"I'm not sure she needs to grow them in greenhouses anymore. They've gone wild outside the courtyard."

"I know. They grew out from under the greenhouses, too, and spread all the way to the pond in the Horse Pasture."

"Do the wild ones glow in the dark?"

"Oh, yes. Pete and I like to take walks around the pond at night now. When the flowers first open they smell so nice."

"Do they give off enough light to keep you from stepping on rattlesnakes?"

"None of us have seen a rattlesnake all spring." Angela glanced nervously at the sky. The dark line rising on the horizon had begun to puff up into cloud shapes. "I have to hurry and put this envelope in the vault."

"What's in it?"

Angela planted a kiss on the envelope. "It's my marriage license. Would you like me to tell you all about the wedding? We'll have time while the roll dough rises."

Lovie checked her watch and dumped Fireball unceremoniously out of her lap. "Dadgum. I forgot the cookies!" Before she reached Granny's kitchen, she could tell it was too late. She donned oven mitts, removed the cookie sheets full of charred lumps from the oven and made a speedy exit to the service porch.

"Angela!" she yelled. "There are ostriches in the dumpster yard!"

"I know," Angela stated matter-of-factly.

Lovie ran back into the mudroom. "What are they for—Granny's nearsighted bird watchers?"

"All of the birders love them. One of our neighbors gave them to Pete when ratite prices dropped so low that he couldn't afford to feed them anymore. Did you know ostriches lay seventy-five eggs a year? We thought it would be fun to serve them to the birders. The trouble is most of the birders are vegetarians."

"I wouldn't eat a ratite egg either. Why is Pete keeping the nasty things so close to the house?"

"He hasn't had time to build a pen tall enough to hold them and they can't run loose because the coyotes will chase them."

"Coyotes, my eye! You'd need a saber-tooth tiger to bring down a bird that big. Why are you gonna marry this Pete guy? His goofy ideas are ruining the ranch. He has birds bigger than Grampa Hank's cows. Think about it, Angela. What kind of a guy gets all worked up over bats and guppies?"

Angela looked downright hostile. "Pete loves this ranch as much as you do, Lovie, and his work is making it better. Granny says so." She held her manila envelope close to her heart and huffed out of the kitchen.

Lovie knew she had better mend the rift before Granny came home. She followed Angela to the study, wondering how to say she was sorry when she was not sorry.

Angela dropped her manila envelope on the desk. She unfolded a wooden stepstool in front of the tall bookcase beside it and climbed up. From the top shelf, she took down a handful of books and handed them to Lovie. "Hold these," she ordered. Then she pressed a button that Lovie could not see and the bookcase swung out of the wall about two inches.

"Wow, why didn't anybody ever tell me this bookcase would do that? I wonder if Mom knows."

"I doubt it. This is Granny's vault." Angela got down and gave Lovie a haughty look and scooted the stepstool out of the way. "This door is very heavy when it's full of books so it has to be opened carefully or the hinges will bend." She slipped her slender fingers into the opening and began to pull.

Thunder gave the amazing bookcase-vault a drum roll by rumbling in the distance. The rumbling quickly grew louder. The windows rattled and another book jiggled off the shelf and hit Angela on the head. Before she could say ouch, a blinding light filled the room, followed by a sharp thunderclap. Angela jumped backward, pulling the vault door wide open. A slippery white apparition flew out. Lovie gasped as it slithered across her face.

Angela let out a shaky laugh. When Lovie opened her eyes, she recognized the ghostly attacker instantly. "What is Mom's wedding gown doing in this vault?"

"It isn't a vault, actually. It's an old cedar closet. The first Lovella stored her hooked rugs in it in the summertime." Angela held the wedding gown's voluminous skirt out of the way so Lovie could see inside. "It still smells like cedar, doesn't it? Granny keeps Mr. Hank's important papers in the bottom drawer so she calls it a vault, but it's really just a cedar closet."

Lovie squatted down and reached out to open the bottom drawer. Angela grabbed her wrist. "We're not allowed in Mr. Hank's things."

Lovie's freckled face turned solid red. She and her mother had been going through Grampa Hank's things for two months. She wondered if he knew. She also wondered if her mother knew about this secret hiding place and she resolved to search through it when Angela was not looking.

She stood up to take a closer look at her mother's wedding gown and ran her hands lovingly over the sumptuous satin. She knew she did not need permission to touch it. It was practically her own. Her mother always told her she would be the only one ever to wear it again. She picked up the hem of the gown's full skirt. "I don't remember Mom's gown having this ruffle."

"Granny had it sewn on for me. I'm taller than your mother. Didn't she tell you I'm wearing your mother's gown to get married in? I think it's prettier with the ruffle, don't you?"

Lovie dropped the ruffle.

"I want you to wear your mother's pink prom dress to my wedding, Lovie."

"What on earth for? I wouldn't be caught dead in that thing. The sleeves are bigger than my head."

"But you have to wear it. Pink is my color. I want you to be my bridesmaid—my only bridesmaid—to surprise Granny. That's why I invited you."

"You invited me—not Grampa Hank? I wanted it to be Grampa Hank. I have to find him to ask....hey wait a minute. Are you telling me you had me frozen or trampled or struck by lightning just so I could come prance around your wedding in some dadgum pink prom dress? What kind of an invitation is that, Angela?"

Angela's dark brown eyes grew darker.

Lovie had a feeling she was about to be in big trouble. She softened her voice and crossed her fingers behind her back. "I didn't mean to upset you, Angela. Don't get all puffed up like some big toad that your fiancé, Pete, would get his jollies out of studying. It's nice that somebody around here wants me for something. Just tell me I don't have to wear the hoop."

Lightning flashed again and the thunder that followed threatened to tear the sky apart. Rain plink, plink, plinked on the porch roof. Angela fled from the study.

"Hey, where are you going?" Lovie called after her.

"To the chapel to see if the river's rising!"

"What are you gonna do about it if it is?"

"Ring the chapel bell to warn Mama!" Angela was getting hysterical.

"Just call her on her cell phone."

"Not everybody has a cell phone, Lovie Grady."

"Then call Grampa Hank's." Lovie picked up the phone on the desk. It was still dead. "Wait, I'm going with you."

"Put my marriage license in the vault first. It goes in the top drawer, or was it the middle one? I don't know. Just drop it in and close the door. Granny doesn't want the vault left open."

"Where will I find you?"

"In the garage. Hurry!"

Lovie brushed the wedding gown out of the way, squatted down and opened the top drawer. It was lined with musty green velvet and was full of small envelopes of seeds with numbers scrawled on them. The middle drawer was labeled, "Deeds," and contained yellowed documents, folded into faded blue folders and tied with faded blue ribbons. The deeds were very old and fragile. She knew that Grampa Hank's will was not among the other documents. Any will that might have included her name could not have been over thirteen years old. Lovie put Angela's marriage license on top of the other documents.

She opened the bottom drawer. Grampa Hank's drawer contained only horse and cattle registration papers and an old photograph. She did not have to read the name on the back of the picture to know who it was. From the many times she had studied the portrait of the first Lovella as a young bride, she knew it was a photograph of her as a young child, a photograph of Little Lovella. If the paper had not been so old and cracked, Lovie would have assumed it was a picture of herself or a twin separated by minutes instead of by generations.

She wondered why this treasure was hidden away in the vault. She had never seen a picture of her great-great-grandmother taken before her neck was scarred by the infamous Comanchero trader. From a dainty chain around Little Lovella's unscarred neck, hung a large filigree cross with a dark oval stone in the middle. It was absolutely, without a doubt, the same cross Maria's husband gave her for a wedding present—the same cross Maria still wore—the same cross that had been buried with the Comanchero.

10

THE CEMETERY

"Lovie!" Angela screamed from the back of the house.

Lovie jumped. She dropped the photograph into the drawer, stuffed the yards and yards of wedding gown back into the cedar-closet vault and closed its bookcase door. She was relieved to hear it click shut. She backed away, marveling at the secret hiding place.

"Dadgum," she groaned. The gown's new ruffle was sticking out of the wall.

"Lovie!"

Shaking her hands in frustration, Lovie hesitated then sprinted down the hall. A monsoon was blowing into the mudroom through the door Angela had left wide open. Lovie could not find a slicker among the chore coats so she threw on a brown canvas jacket with a broken zipper and grabbed a wilted cap with the stiff logo of an animal health company. She ran down the steps of the service porch. The ostriches rotated their heads toward her in unison. They looked miserable, standing outside the temporary awning that had been erected for their protection.

Angela was sitting behind the wheel of Granny's silver *Cadillac* when Lovie burst into the garage. She wore a clear plastic poncho and rain cap that looked like they had come out of Granny's glove compartment. Lovie knocked on the tinted window.

Angela lowered the window an inch. "Don't just stand there, Lovie. Get in." Angela revved the *Cadillac's* big motor.

"Did you say you're going to the chapel?" Lovie hollered.

"Yes. We can see the river from there. Get in."

"Are you nuts? We can't drive Granny's car through the mud. She'll tan our hides."

Angela glared at her defiantly and cut the engine. "We'll take Pete's jeep then. It's in the machine shed." She pushed Lovie aside with the car door and raced out into the pounding rain.

Lovie hoped her cap was waterproof. She pushed the button to lower the garage door and ducked under it before it crushed her, then she splashed through the downpour after Angela.

The machine shed was an open-faced pole barn where Grampa Hank used to park his trailers, spray rig, cake wagon, and an old broken down tractor that had not seen the light of day in Lovie's lifetime. Since the crew had taken most of the equipment to the River Camp, the shed was practically empty. All that was left behind was the dusty tractor and whatever was under the tarp Angela was struggling with.

Angela was nearly in tears. "I can't get this tarp off. It's caught on something."

Lovie calmly unhooked the bungee cords and lifted the tarp to reveal an ancient purple jeep with nothing over the cab but a crudely welded roll bar. Angela jerked the tarp out of her hands and threw it aside.

"Do you know how to drive this thing?" Lovie asked.

"Of course I do. Pete showed me. Now get in!"

Lovie climbed in over the side. There was no door to open. The floorboard was rusted out and the dirt floor of the machine shed showed through a gaping hole. There was just enough room for Lovie to put one foot on either side. "This is handy, Angela. When it rains in the top, the water can't collect around your feet."

Angela started the jeep. She tried all four gears several times trying to find one that did not grind. Then she did what she said Pete usually did. She turned the key off, put the shifting lever in reverse and started it up again. But her wet foot slipped off the clutch and the jeep shot backwards, nearly ejecting Lovie who did not have the benefit of a steering wheel to hold onto.

They backed out onto the gravel road between the main house and the barns. Angela managed to get the jeep out of reverse and forced it into first gear. It lurched forward then crawled along at a snail's pace. The ostriches stood in the rain in single file, like chorus girls, and watched it go by. Angela gunned the motor and shoved the lever into second without too much grinding.

They picked up speed past the arena and round corral. Lovie

pointed to one of the light poles which was splintered and missing its lights. "Look! That's where the lightning struck!"

They crossed the cattleguard into the Camposanto Pasture and picked up more speed going downhill toward the creek. The windshield wiper worked, but it did not help Angela see through the rain that was falling inside the open-topped vehicle. The nearer she got to the creek, the faster she drove. She did not seem to care that water was running over the road.

Lovie held onto her seat cushion for dear life. "You might want to slow it down going through the water," she suggested. "I'm not sure these old cushions will work for floatation devices."

Angela hit the water going the speed of light. Water splashed higher than the cottonwood trees. The jeep stalled out in the middle of the creek.

"That's slow enough," Lovie said. Glowing white blossoms floated by beneath the hole in the floorboard. "Granny's flowers have spread all the way to the creek. They sure must like water. Do you want me to scoop you up a bouquet?"

"This isn't funny, Lovie." Angela tried to start the engine again but it would not cooperate. She pulled on the choke, mashed on the starter button with her toe, and held the gas pedal all the way to the floor with her heel. The jeep cranked and cranked but there was no ignition.

"You're gonna wear down the battery," Lovie cautioned. "The distributor is probably wet." She poked her jeans into her boots and climbed out into the water. Holding onto the jeep, she waded forward to open the hood. With the sleeve of her jacket, she unsnapped the distributor cap. Angela sat in the driver's seat gripping the steering wheel. There was nothing else she could do.

Lovie pulled a pair of cotton roping gloves out of her jacket pocket and used them to dry the distributor. "It smells like something died out here. It must be something big to smell so bad in all this rain. Okay, it's dry. Try to start it again."

It worked. The jeep coughed and trembled and lurched forward again. Lovie jumped in before she was left standing in the middle of the creek. The current pushed the jeep sideways. Then its wheels grabbed the rocky creek bottom and pulled itself out of the water.

"Stop, Angela! There is something dead." Lovie stood up and grabbed onto the roll bar for a better look.

Angela tugged on her arm. "Sit down! Sit down!"

"Look over there! It's one of Grampa Hank's yearling bulls." Lovie jumped out of the moving jeep and ran over to the still mound of black hair. The dead bull was lying on his side with his legs sticking straight out and his head stretched back. The edge of the creek lapped at his nostrils.

"Did he drown?" Angela pumped the brake until the jeep stopped.

"Cattle don't drown in creeks this shallow. I don't know what happened to him."

Angela looked like she was going to be sick. "Can we go now, please?"

Lovie was surprised at her total lack of sympathy for the poor young bull. She made a mental note of the animal's ear tag number and hip brand for Grampa Hank and climbed back into the jeep.

Angela caught a gear and took off up the hill.

"Why are you so freaked out about the river rising? Grampa Hank won't let anybody cross if he thinks it's too high. He'll make them take the long way around and cross over the highway bridge."

"When Mr. Hank has cattle on his mind, nothing else gets through to him. Granny says so."

They crossed the cattleguard into the church yard and started to circle in front of the chapel. Angela suddenly cranked the wheel the other way and detoured between the chapel and the cemetery. The jeep began to slip and slide on the bare ground. Lovie did not have to ask if it was in four wheel drive. She could tell by the way it was handling that it was not.

"Where are you going, Angela?"

"We'd better park at the very top of the hill, like Pete does, in case we have to give the jeep a push to start it."

"What makes you think we can push it in this mud?"

The jeep swerved and made ruts through a patch of wild irises. In spite of herself, Lovie looked for Granny and Grampa Hank's graves. They would not be hard to spot, even in the rain. Their matching headstones were tall and shiny and the wings of their angels were not broken like some of the older ones. But their headstones were not there, as though the angels had carried them away.

"You're almost there," Lovie encouraged. "When we stop, I'll show you how to lock the hubs and put it in four wheel drive." It crossed her mind that it might be safer to tie Angela in the rumble seat and drive Pete's jeep back to headquarters herself.

Instead of chewing its way forward to the top of the hill, the jeep started sliding backward. Angela screamed when the rear wheel on Lovie's side dropped into a hole. The front wheel on Angela's side lifted off the ground and slung mud at her. Lovie grabbed onto the frame of the windshield and prayed that the little buggy would not tip over backward.

It stayed put.

She climbed out carefully, thankful to have her feet back on the muddy ground, and turned around to survey the damage. To her horror, the jeep's right hind tire was planted deeply among the purple irises of the Comanchero's sunken grave. She clamped her wet hands over her mouth but Grampa Hank's string of cusswords still escaped.

Angela had no idea what was wrong, only that it must be something very bad. She stomped on the gas pedal. The back wheels spun unproductively, doing little more than possibly adding tire tracks to the Comanchero's skull—which the first Lovella's mother had already marked with a bullet hole over a century before.

11

THE CHAPEL

In their vain attempt to get traction, the jeep's rear tires pelted Lovie with mud clods. "Stop gunning it, Angela! Stop! You'll make it turn over!"

Angela could not hear Lovie's pleas over the whining of the engine. Lovie tore around to the driver's side, locked her arms around Angela's slender body and tried to pull her out of harm's way. Angela tightened her grip on the wheel. With no time to reason with her, Lovie let out a groan like a Sumo wrestler and jerked the petrified girl out of the driver's seat with all her might. Angela landed face down in the mud, safely away from the doomed jeep.

Pete's purple jeep flipped over on its top, driving its roll bar into the rain-softened ground at the foot of the Comanchero's grave, covering it like a fallen tombstone. The engine shuddered, coughed and died. The rain hammered on its rusty belly.

All Angela could do was sob. "Look what you did to Pete's beautiful jeep. Why did you have to make it turn over?"

"I didn't make it turn over. You did. And it was about to turn over with you in it. So stop bawling. You're lucky this rusty old piece of junk didn't pin you in the grave with the Comanchero."

Angela's sobbing stopped abruptly. She picked herself out of the mud and wiped her face on the sleeve of her muddy white blouse. "To you, it's a rusty old piece of junk but it's Pete's rusty old piece of junk so I love it. Not everyone can afford a *Land Rover*."

The clouds were churning into the peanut shapes characteristic of an eminent hailstorm.

"I'm sorry about Pete's jeep, Angela. But right now I don't know what to do about it and I don't feel like hanging around a graveyard in a hailstorm, trying to figure it out."

Lovie took off for the safety of the chapel. She flushed out a cottontail in her path, making the day stressful for an animal that spends its nights dodging owls and coyotes. The chapel bell droned as hailstones began to pummel it.

Angela reached the chapel first. She lifted the door latch, slipped inside and slammed the heavy double doors in Lovie's face. Lovie heard her throw the bolt over the latch on the inside. She was locked out.

She discovered that nothing she had on was waterproof, certainly not hail proof. She kicked the doors as hard as she could, but dislodged only the mud caked on her boots. She leaned her face against the weathered wood and rounded her back against the hailstones. The chapel bell began to ring in earnest. She covered her ears. When the bell ringing finally stopped and the ringing in her ears became bearable, the door latch popped up and the door opened.

In spite of the hail, Lovie hesitated to enter the chapel. Angela stood in the doorway holding the end of a long rope. "The bell pull broke," she said. "Don't bother to tell Granny. Pete can fix it." She dropped the rope in front of Lovie and turned and walked regally down the aisle between the rows of crude benches, practicing the halting steps of a bride in a procession.

Lovie caught up with her near the altar and reached out to grab a hank of her long hair, but before she could lay a hand on her, Angela dropped to her knees and slumped over the altar rail. Before Lovie could rationalize doing bodily harm to someone kneeling at an altar, Angela began talking to a cardboard box on the other side of the rail.

"Hello sweet things," she cooed. Two fluffy white heads peeked over the top of the box and whimpered. Up popped two more—then two more. The box bubbled over with fluffy white puppies.

Lovie peered into the box in amazement. "…three, four, five…" she counted. "There are seven of them. Where did they come from?"

"Pete found them in the thicket in an ice storm. And don't you dare tell Granny they're here. We've been moving them from place to place so she won't find them. Pete's trying to convince Mr. Hank to let us keep them. He loves dogs."

That was the first sensible thing Lovie had heard about Pete. "It's a good thing he loves them. These are Great Pyrenees puppies. I know because Grampa Hank had one once. You're fixing to have seven dogs that weigh more than you do."

"I know we won't be able to keep them all. Mr. Hank said he'd take two of them to the River Camp for us and try to find homes for the rest. Aren't they sweet? Pete's been bottle-feeding them every four hours. We don't know what happened to their mother."

Lovie picked up a fluffy white female and held it to her cheek. She looked into the puppy's soft brown eyes, rimmed in black as though someone had made her up with eyeliner. She had Cotton's face. She licked Lovie tentatively on the tip of her nose. Lovie put her back in the box and picked up a little male. He had Cotton's face too. They all had Cotton's face. *I bet I know where their mother is,"* Lovie thought.

Angela lifted the lid of the baptismal font and took out a box of matches. Except when it was to be filled with water for a baptism, Granny stored matches there to keep the mice from chewing them up. While Lovie pet the wriggling puppies, Angela struck matches and lit candles. First she lit the candles in the two freestanding candelabras that a long-ago ranch hand had fashioned out of horseshoes. Then she moved to the votive candles on the small table beneath a stained glass window of Saint Francis, the patron saint of animals.

The sweet scent of the votives reached Lovie's nostrils, courtesy of a cold draft blowing the flames away from the window. Although the flickering candles made the room look warmer, the negligible amount of heat they generated escaped through the rafters. Angela lit the last candle and gazed into it with a dour expression. It spewed and popped and went out.

Lovie put the puppies back in the box. "If you're trying to warm these pups with all those candles, you're wasting your time."

"I'm lighting them for Mama, to keep her safe. You wouldn't understand. Mama said you're a Protestant."

"What of it? Are you prejudiced?" Lovie retrieved a box of matches from the font and dragged the box of puppies to a small corner fireplace at the back of the chapel. "I might not understand everything that's going on around here, but what I do know is that these puppies are cold. They need a fire." She struck a match and lit the kindling that had been carefully placed there. "This way we can warm the pups and send smoke signals to Maria at the same time."

Angela gave Lovie a look colder than the room. "Why do you have to make a joke of everything? I'm worried about Mama. Have you ever cared about anyone but yourself?"

The hail had stopped bouncing around the churchyard and was melting in the deluge that followed. As much as Lovie wanted to get away from Angela, she did not relish running back to headquarters through the downpour. She was cold enough already. And she knew she would have to endure Granny's wrath if she did not try to put a smile back on Angela's face.

"You never finished telling me about your wedding, Angela," Lovie said sweetly.

"Why do you care?"

Lovie crossed her fingers. "I care. I really do. I love hearing about weddings."

"I don't believe you but..." But since brides-to-be cannot resist talking about their weddings, she continued. "My cousin and his two little kids are coming to the rehearsal dinner tomorrow night. I'm excited about that. I'm also excited because Granny is planning a surprise for me. Pete knows what it is but he won't tell me. My bouquet will be made of Granny's glow-in-the-dark flowers and you will carry her pink long-stemmed bluebonnets. Her blue bluebonnets are my *something blue.* Your mother's wedding gown is *something borrowed.* For *something old,* Mama is letting me wear the ruby cross Papa gave her when they got married."

Lovie knew it would be a bad time to ask Angela how her Papa got his hands on her great-great-grandmother Lovella's cross in the first place. Trying not to sound resentful, she asked, "Is Granny letting you borrow my mother's mantilla, too?"

"Your mother borrowed the mantilla from Mama. It came from Mexico. Mama wore it when she married Papa, but Mama's dress is too small for me. She was very thin."

Lovie could not imagine anybody thinner than Angela. "I didn't know the mantilla was your mother's. I didn't even know my mother knew yours until Maria told me."

"How like your mother not to mention that she knew mine."

"What do you mean by that? My mother knows a lot of people. She doesn't tell me about all of them."

"Mama grew up on the Crossover Ranch. My grandfather was the chuck wagon cook when the wagon crew used to stay out working cattle for a month at a time. Your mother never told you that, did she? Your mother and mine went to school together until your mother went to private school. When your mother got engaged, she asked my mother to be the matron of honor, but she changed her mind because her sorority sisters made fun of her for having a cook's daughter in the wedding party. I'll bet she never told you that either. Mama let her wear her mantilla anyway because it looked so beautiful with your mother's gown. Papa told me that a long time ago, before you were born. Think about that before you call me 'prejudiced' again."

Lovie was speechless. She couldn't imagine her mother doing something like that. It made the things she was always mad at her mother for seem trivial. She left the box of puppies sleeping by the fireplace and went and stood quietly by the votive candles. She stared out the stained glass window, looking for answers that were not there. She knew it was not her own fault if her mother had done such a mean thing to Maria but it made her feel guilty anyway. She re-lit the candle that had gone out. It struggled to stay lit in the draft that was coming through the leaded outlines of Saint Francis' red glass birds and clear glass sheep.

The candles began to give off an unpleasant odor. Instead of the draft blowing the candle flames away from the window, the flames began to be drawn toward it instead. Saint Francis' flock of glass birds and sheep began to vibrate. Lovie put her hand against one of the clear glass sheep to steady it. A hand met hers on the other side.

Lovie was unable to pull her own hand away. She felt the same sensation as when she stuck a magnet to the refrigerator door that her mother had gotten out of a fried hard drive. They could not use it to stick notes to the refrigerator because it was too hard to pull off.

Lovie watched El Lobo's shadow draw close to the window and she was repulsed by the stench of dead skunk. The scar between his eyes burned red when he pressed his forehead against a red glass bird. Lovie screamed and the hand on the other side of the glass was withdrawn, releasing hers.

She raced down the aisle toward the double doors. "Angela! Barricade the doors! Barricade the doors!"

Angela did not budge. "What for? Aren't we a little old to be playing Alamo?"

"I'm not playing!" Lovie lunged at the door and threw the bolt over the latch herself. She leaned hard against it and felt someone knocking on the other side. The knocking turned to pounding. "Don't just stand there. Help me! El Lobo is out there. I saw him at the window. He's still following me!"

"He's here? Let him in, Lovie." Angela shoved Lovie with the strength a stick-thin girl should not possess.

"Angela, don't! El Lobo is evil!"

"He is not evil. El Lobo is my Papa—El Lobo Lopez. He's come to walk me down the aisle." Angela yanked open the chapel doors, prepared to throw herself into the arms of the evil man on the other side.

But El Lobo was nowhere to be seen.

"Pete! It's you." Angela threw herself into the arms of her startled fiancé instead.

12

PETE

Pete freed himself from Angela, self-consciously, and pushed her gently out from under the water dripping off the roof. The rain squall had moved on. Lovie stood in the threshold waiting to see if El Lobo would make his presence known. She was certain it had been El Lobo peering at her through the red stained glass and not Angela's red-faced fiancé.

Once inside the chapel, Pete removed his wet hat. His thick hair was as red as Lovie's and it remained dented where his hat's sweatband fit snugly, giving him the appearance of having a deformed head. He noticed Lovie's hair right away and smiled the smile reserved for fellow survivors of grade school names like carrot-top and flame-brain. When Pete smiled, the dimples in his sunburned cheeks sank in so far he could have hidden his lunch money in them.

Angela slipped her arm through Pete's. Pete looked down at her and took out his handkerchief to wipe away the dirt left on her face. "Looks like y'all have been mud wrestling," he said.

Angela brushed the handkerchief away. "Pete, did Mama make it back alright?"

"Sure. Why wouldn't she?"

"It rained so hard I was afraid the river would be dangerous to cross, so I rang the bell to warn her—and you of course. Did you hear it?"

"Sure did. I thought y'all must be trying to scare the bats out of the bell tower. It didn't rain a drop at the River Camp. I'm kinda glad, too, 'cause we sprayed the cattle for horn flies and the rain woulda washed it all off. That dang chemical spray costs an arm and a leg. I'm trying to get Mr. Hank to propagate dung beetles to keep the horn fly population down."

Lovie did not want to talk about horn flies and dung beetles. "Excuse me, but did Grampa Hank come back with you?"

"No, Ma'am." Pete held out his hand. "I'm Pete Upchurch, Ma'am."

Angela leaned closer to Pete. "This is Mr. Hank's granddaughter, Lovie Grady. I invited her to be my bridesmaid..." Pete's green eyes met Lovie's green eyes. "...for our wedding," Angela continued.

"Pleased to meet you, Lovie. Y'all picked a rough day to drive up to the chapel. I saw my jeep belly-up by the cemetery."

"Oh, Pete," Angela said with a catch in her throat. "I'm so sorry about your beautiful jeep. Lovie didn't mean to wreck it."

"Me?" said Lovie.

Pete surveyed Lovie from the tip of her freckled nose to the tips of her muddy boots and back. "Are you hurt, Lovie?"

Angela pulled Pete away from Lovie. "We're both fine. Your jeep slid off the road and Lovie pulled me out of it so hard that it flipped all the way over and then..." And then Angela started bawling.

It was too much for Pete. Worry lines creased his forehead. He patted Angela on the back. She buried her face in his denim shirt. He patted her harder.

It was too much for Lovie, too, but she decided not to ruin the tender moment by mentioning that when the jeep slid off the road, it dug up the grave of the long dead Comanchero. "Pete, did you see anybody outside when you drove up? I thought I saw somebody at the window."

Angela stopped crying and mouthed a silent sh-h-h to Lovie. Lovie did not blame her for not wanting to talk about her skunk of a Papa.

"No, Ma'am," Pete answered. "Just y'all."

"Well I'm sorry about your jeep. Want me to send somebody up here to help you with it? I'm taking the shortcut back to headquarters."

Angela waved her away. "We don't need any help. Do we Pete?" Pete shrugged his shoulders.

"*Great,*" Lovie thought as she left the chapel. "*Nobody on this ranch wants my help except Mom and I don't even know where she is.*"

The view across the river from the chapel hill was spectacular. The red canyon wall on the south side of the river was a perfect contrast to the green trees along the river banks. "*Red and green,*" thought Lovie. "*If I don't wake up from this dream of Granny's, I'm gonna miss Christmas. Please, let it be a dream.*"

She trotted down the footpath toward the creek in the thicket. She had no desire to return by way of the road—and the dead bull. Two keen-scented buzzards were already circling the vicinity of the carcass.

The trees that grew along the creek formed an umbrella over the narrow wooden footbridge. Granny's glow-in-the-dark flowers had gone wild in a big way where the shade was thickest. Lovie leaned over the handrail and watched rain-battered blossoms float by on ripples of water headed to the river.

She used to sit on the bridge in the summertime, dangling her feet in the water, while Dingo and Cotton splashed through the creek. They seemed to enjoy running up to within inches of her and shaking cold water all over her. She missed them. They made her feel safe. She looked back up the path to make sure El Lobo was not following her. "*If El Lobo is Angela's father,*" she thought, "*and Maria is Angela's mother then El Lobo is Maria's husband. Where is the little girl that drowned with Maria?*" She shivered at the thought of Maria and her little girl being swept down the river by the flash flood.

Lovie found Granny planting flowers by the gazebo. The carpenters were doing their best to work around her. "Wow, Granny. Your gazebo is almost finished!" Lovie said.

"It had better be," Granny said loud enough for the carpenters to hear plainly. "Angela wants to use it tomorrow morning for her bridesmaid's luncheon."

"Then it doesn't really matter. I'm the only bridesmaid and I don't care where we eat, just so we eat."

"How can you be the bridesmaid, Lovella? Angela didn't even know you were coming until last night."

"Well actually..." Lovie tried to think of a diplomatic way to tell Granny that Angela had her frozen or trampled or struck by lightning to get her here. "Actually, the reason I turned up at the cookhouse unexpectedly last night was because Angela invited me to be in her wedding. The invitation didn't come in the mail or anything. It's sort of a command performance."

Granny put down her shovel and gave her mud-splattered granddaughter a skeptical look. "Oh...I wish she had asked me first. Do you have something suitable to wear?"

"Well, since I didn't show up with a suitcase full of the latest in bridesmaid's attire, she wants me to wear Mom's old pink prom dress."

Granny raised her eyebrows. "Are you quite sure?"

"Quite sure. Pathetic, huh? Speaking of pathetic—did you know there's a dead yearling bull on the road to the chapel?" Lovie pointed toward the creek. "See the buzzards flying around?"

"Your grandfather promised he'd move them all to the other side of the river before the wedding. We can't have wedding guests going past dead animals to get to the chapel. I'll have to speak to Pete about it." Granny picked up a peat pot and handed it to Lovie. "You'll have to plant the rest of these. The hardest part is keeping the carpenters from stepping on them as fast as you plant them." The carpenters looked up.

"Granny, wait. Pete's at the chapel. So is El Lobo. He was peeking in the stained glass window at me. I told you he was following me."

"Nonsense, Lovella! El Lobo hasn't been near the chapel since his wedding day."

"I know now why Maria is afraid of him."

"Then you know more than you have any business knowing."

"El Lobo is Maria's husband, isn't he? She helped him steal Grampa Hank's cattle and she got stuck in the river and drowned."

The carpenters stopped hammering. With a sidelong glance at them, Granny walked away. "El Lobo forced her to help him, Lovella. If you don't mind, I'd rather not discuss this with you."

Lovie did mind. She ran and stood in front of her grandmother. "It isn't Grampa Hank's fault that Maria and her little girl drowned. He fired a warning shot."

"That gunshot cost Maria and her precious little girl their lives."

"But Maria is here with you. Where's the little girl?"

"The little girl is here with me, too. Her name is Angela. She grew up, Lovella. Maria's daughter had a right to grow up and have a beautiful wedding, just as my daughter did. Her life should not have been wasted on a bunch of stolen cows. I'm giving Angela a surprise wedding gift at her rehearsal dinner to make up for the misery our family has caused hers."

"Grampa Hank is fixing up the old homestead ruin under Buzzard Point. Is that your gift?"

"You can't be serious. That old house is not a sufficient sacrifice. I've decided to give her the entire Crossover Ranch."

"You can't give her the ranch. Grampa Hank promised it to me and I want it. It's my dream. I'll fall into the bottomless pit of hopelessness without it and I don't even know where the bottomless pit of hopelessness is. But I guess I'm fixing to find out because you're giving my dream away to a bunch of dead people!"

The carpenters were staring at them with stricken looks on their faces. Granny no longer seemed aware of their presence. "I'll thank you to keep a civil tongue in your head, Mary Lovella Grady. Jealously does not become you. Like it or not, it is your duty as a member of this family to make up for the tragedy we have inflicted on Angela."

"I haven't inflicted anything on her...yet."

A ranch pickup splashed across the creek, towing Pete's purple jeep. More buzzards than before took to the air and spiraled over the location of the dead bull. Lovie shuddered, less from the sight of the buzzards than from the rain soaked clothes that were chilling her to the bone.

13

THE PROM DRESS

The jeep's roll bar was at a forty-five degree angle. With every jerk of the log chain that attached it to the ranch pickup, globs of mud splatted onto its seats.

Granny looked suspiciously at Lovie. "Why would Pete be towing his jeep?"

Before Lovie could answer, Maria came running from the cookhouse. "Mary Lovella! Where is Angela? I cannot find her anywhere. I am so worried. I saw the black cloud."

"She's probably in the machine shed with Pete. She got the jeep stuck in the mud and Pete had to tow it back."

"Honestly, Lovella," Granny said. "Angela is much too busy preparing for her wedding to be giving you jeep rides."

"It wasn't my idea. Angela freaked out when it started raining, just like you said she would, Maria."

Granny pinched Lovie's arm.

Lovie flinched but kept talking. "She wanted to warn you that the river might be rising so she drove Pete's jeep up to the chapel to ring the bell and she ran over that sunken grave with all the wild irises..." Granny and Maria both gasped. "...and the jeep flipped over on top of it. But nobody got hurt—except maybe the Comanchero."

Angela called to her mother from the back porch of main house and collapsed into the porch swing. Her eyes narrowed when she saw Lovie. Maria and Granny rushed to her side. "Lovie told you about the grave, didn't she?"

Granny tried to soothe her. "This is not a pleasant subject, Angela, dear. Let's go inside and talk about your wedding preparations instead. I haven't seen you in your gown since the seamstress added the new ruffle.

Maybe you could let us sample a few of your cookies—not the ones I found on the service porch, however. I suspect Lovella had something to do with those. You didn't let her near your roll dough did you?"

"My roll dough!" Angela groaned. "It must be all over the counter by now." Angela bolted for the cookhouse. Maria ran after her.

Lovie made a move in that direction but Granny stopped her. "You've done enough, Lovella. Go upstairs and clean yourself up. I'll find your mother's prom dress so you can try it on. It's important to me that we make Angela happy. Do you understand?"

"No, I do not understand. I do not understand anything that's going on around here except that the happier we make Angela, the unhappier we make me. Do I have to wear that old thing?"

"If that is the dress Angela wants you to wear in her wedding, then that is the dress you'll wear." Granny picked up the end of Lovie's matted ponytail. "There must be something we can do with this hair. Would you like me to cut it for you?"

Lovie pulled her hair out of Granny's hand. "No way! I like being able to tie it back out of my face when I ride."

"I think it's more feminine left loose. Maybe you could try curling it on large rollers to straighten it out a little for the wedding. It looks unkempt, all skinned back with those kinky things popping out." Granny unconsciously tucked her own kinky things back into her bun.

Lovie went upstairs and showered in the pink bathroom next to her mother's pink bedroom. She covered her camouflage-colored underwear with a short pink bathrobe that was hanging in the bathroom and wrapped a pink towel around her head. She hated pink.

Granny came in with the pink prom dress draped over her arm. It did not seem as fluffy as it had in the photograph on the grand piano. Age made the multiple layers of lace limp and droopy. The smattering of sequins that sparkled years ago were now dull and gray.

Lovie sat down on the bed. "Granny, you can't be serious. It looks more like a Halloween costume."

Granny tried to fluff the skirt. "Maybe it won't be so bad if we cut off the sequins and give it a good steaming. It was made to wear over a hoopskirt, you know. I'll go find it."

"No possible way am I gonna wear a hoopskirt. I'll look like the cake topper."

"Maybe a stiff petticoat? Just try it on and we'll see. But first dry your hair and put on these pantyhose. Call me when it's time to zip you. I'm going downstairs to make tea."

Lovie dried her hair with an ancient hair dryer she found in a vanity drawer. It blew scorching hot air at about two hundred miles per hour. When her fine curly hair was dry, it stuck up all over her head like a Halloween wig. She did not attempt to tie it back, but left it "loose" like Granny wanted—really loose.

She opted out of putting on the pantyhose. It was too hot and humid, and the dress was too long for Granny to be able to see if she was wearing them or not. She dropped the dress on the floor in front of her, stepped into the hole in the middle and pulled it up to her waist. It itched. It smelled funny. Reluctantly, she eased her arms into the huge puffed sleeves. They were the only things on the dress that did not droop. They stuck up past her ears.

She could not begin to get it zipped. Her waist was bigger than her mother's had been at her age and the skin-tight bodice refused to wrap all the way around her. She sucked in her tummy till her eyes bulged, but it was no use.

Holding the zipper together with one hand behind her back, she maneuvered down the hall with the back of her camouflage colored sports bra showing plainly. Without a petticoat to hold up the layers of ruffles, the skirt dragged on the floor and she kept stepping on it.

Granny was waiting at the bottom of the stairs. She had changed into a mauve silk blouse and decked out in turquoise jewelry for the tea party. She pursed her lips when she saw her granddaughter. The limpness of the long lace dress was emphasized by its huge sleeves and Lovie's huge hair.

Lovie's grand entrance ended when she stepped on the skirt and ripped out its gathered waist from one side of the bodice to the other. She continued to clutch the zipper together behind her and grabbed the banister with her free hand to keep from landing on top of Granny at the bottom of the stairs. To Granny's horror, the skirt's drooping waist framed Lovie's camouflage briefs.

"Whoops," Lovie said. She hoisted the layers of limp ruffles and turned around to retreat, giving Granny one last glimpse of her camo undie ensemble through the unzipped bodice of the ruined prom dress.

Back in the bedroom, she stuffed the torn dress through a sagging hanger and shoved it in the closet. "Yes!" she hissed, bringing her fist down in a triumphant gesture. She was confident that the dress could not be resurrected for such a public event as a wedding. She gladly donned her dirty blue jeans and alien t-shirt and slid down the banister to hurry up and get the tongue-lashing she anticipated from Granny over with. This Granny was sure grouchier than the grouchy Granny she used to love. At least that Granny loved her back.

Granny and Maria sat in matching wingback chairs in the formal living room, sipping tea from porcelain teacups. On the wall behind them were two large, dark, oil paintings of Granny's parents with eyes that scowled at Lovie as she walked through the room. Even with the drapes open and the picture lights on, the living room had a somber look to match the expressions in the paintings. It made Lovie feel like whispering. She understood why Grampa Hank always hung out in his den instead.

"I'm sorry about the dress, Granny," Lovie lied softly.

"So am I, Lovella. I'm sure you would have made a lovely bridesmaid in it," Granny lied in return.

"It is alright, *m'ija*," consoled Maria. "We'll find you another one."

Lovie looked at Granny but neither of them said a thing.

Angela strode silently across the soft carpet, carrying the wedding gown. She kissed Maria and then Granny and smiled at them radiantly, exhibiting perfectly straight teeth that had never seen an orthodontist. "Lovie, as my bridesmaid, you may help me with my dress."

"Let your mother help you, dear," Granny suggested. "It might be safer."

Maria was more than agreeable to play lady-in-waiting and escorted Angela up to Granny's room to help her with her gown. Lovie settled unceremoniously into Maria's vacant chair and brought her bare feet up underneath her.

"Don't put your feet on the furniture, Lovella," Granny said. "Angela seems to have recovered from her encounter with the Comanchero's grave, don't you think?"

"I guess so. Granny, why is the Comanchero buried outside our family cemetery?"

"That's as far as my great-grandmother had the strength to drag him after she shot him. My great-grandfather wasn't home at the time. He'd gone after the cattle the rest of the Comanchero band had stolen. Little Lovella, my grandmother, had to help her mother bury the thief. When they rolled him into his grave, he was still clutching Little Lovella's cross in one hand and his Bowie knife in the other—the good with the bad—just like all of us."

"I think your great-grandmother should have dragged him to Buzzard Point and fed him the buzzards, for trying to kidnap her little girl."

"She shot him for it. That was enough. He might have only wanted her cross. We'll never know."

"About that cross..." Lovie began.

Someone knocked on the front door. "Excuse me, Lovella," Granny interrupted and went to answer it.

Lovie heard Pete's voice and went to see. Pete was standing in the front hall in his stocking feet, having taken off his muddy boots on the porch. He nodded to her shyly and tried not to stare at her hair.

Granny talked to him in a low voice. "Merciful heavens, Pete. Are you quite sure there was nothing else in that grave? Nothing at all?"

"Only this feather, Ma'am. It's the craziest thing. I pulled my jeep out of that grave, expecting to find a skeleton with a skull fracture. But there was nothing left in it but this dang buzzard feather."

Granny backed away from it.

"Uh...do you want me to cover the grave back up, Ma'am?" Pete stuttered. He could not take his eyes off of Lovie's wild red hair.

Lovie could not take her eyes off the feather.

"Yes, Pete, please cover it up," Granny responded. "And thank you for telling me."

"Pete!" Maria shrieked from the upstairs landing. "What are you doing here, *m'ijo*? You are not allowed to see Angela in her wedding dress. It is a bad omen. Go away. Go!"

Pete shrugged his shoulders at Granny apologetically and hastened to follow the instructions of his future mother-in-law. He tossed the feather to Lovie and left.

Maria proudly led Angela out of Granny's bedroom. Angela looked stunning. She held her head like a princess and descended the stairs without once tripping on the wedding gown's new ruffle. Unlike Lovie's dress, the only things showing beneath Angela's were the toes of her satin slippers.

She was wearing Maria's ruby cross. She covered it with her hand when she noticed Lovie looking at it so strangely. "Look, Lovie. Mama gave me her cross, the cross Papa gave her. It's my something old, remember?"

"You can't have that cross, Angela".

"Lovella!" Granny snapped. "Mind your manners."

"It belongs to my family, not yours. The Comanchero took it from Little Lovella."

"You think everything in the world belongs to your family, Lovie Grady."

"I can prove it. I saw a picture in the vault of Little Lovella wearing that very same cross. How did your Papa get his hands on it?" Lovie turned to Granny. "You and Grampa Hank must have known that El Lobo gave Maria your grandmother's cross."

"Yes, we knew it, Lovella. We didn't know how he got it and we didn't want to know. Maria was so pleased that El Lobo gave her something of religious significance. I'm so very sorry, Maria. We hid the picture of Little Lovella wearing the cross so you wouldn't find out that it was the cross the Comanchero cut off Little Lovella's necklace so long ago."

Granny put her arm around Maria who was going weak in the knees. "Maria is the kindest person I've ever known, Lovella. She deserved to wear that cross, no matter whose it was originally."

"And now it's mine," Angela spewed, her face darkening with rage.

"Your precious Papa robbed a grave to get it, Angela. The truth is as plain as the perfect nose on your perfect face. Who do you think left this buzzard feather in the Comanchero's grave? Who leaves buzzard feathers everywhere he goes, like he's molting or something? El Lobo, your Papa." Lovie brushed the long black feather under Angela's nose.

Angela slapped it away like a biting fly then aimed her open palm at Lovie's face. Maria grabbed her around her tiny waist and held her back. "No, m'ija!"

"I hate you, Lovie Grady! I hate you!" Angela screamed, straining to get away. "I don't want such a hateful girl in my wedding."

"Why did you invite me here then? I'd way rather be trekking through boring art galleries in Santa Fe with Mom and Dad than hanging around here with you."

"I didn't want to invite you. I wanted to invite Papa. Papa promised to walk me down the aisle when I was a little girl. But Mama and Granny wouldn't let me. They think he's evil but he's not, not to me. So I invited you because I knew Papa was following you."

Maria let go of Angela and crossed herself. *"Madre de Dios.* Can it be true? El Lobo is really here?"

Granny tried to comfort her. "It's alright, Maria. We'll go to the chapel and light candles tonight—as many as you want." Granny led Maria back to the teapot.

Angela scowled at Lovie. "Now you've done it, you spoiled brat. I have to tell Pete to hide the puppies." Angela lifted the skirt of the heavy satin gown and bounded up the stairs. She spun around at the top. "Do you remember when you used to play Alamo in the chapel with your imaginary friend? Well I wasn't imaginary. You always got to play Davy Crockett, remember? And you thought I was playing Jim Bowie, but I tricked you. I was Generalisimo Santa Ana. Do you remember what Santa Ana's army did to Davy Crockett at the Alamo?"

14

BUZZARD POINT

Lovie sat on the floor of her mother's bedroom, wrapped in a down comforter, even though it was June. Everyone was angry with her. It made her feel awful. She wondered if she had made her mother feel so awful by being angry with her the last couple of months. She wished she could tell her she was sorry. She wondered if her mother had ever told Maria she was sorry.

Someone beat the triangle at the cookhouse. The bunkhouse doors flew open and boots scooted across the breezeway to answer its call but no one asked her to come down for supper.

Just after sundown, Lovie heard Granny leave the house. Her voice mingled with the others who were busy filling luminaria sacks with sand and candles to light the path to the chapel. Pete and the ranch hands had spent the afternoon festooning the trees in the thicket with tiny white lights, powered by solar batteries. The bridal procession would follow the candlelit footpath through the twinkling thicket to the chapel on the evening of the wedding. Guests would be taken up the gravel road in horse-drawn wagons by lantern light. Afterward, the newlyweds would lead everyone back to the courtyard for dinner and dancing.

The voices drifted farther and farther from the courtyard until they were drowned out by a pack of coyotes, announcing that it was time to chase the cats and poultry around the barnyards of the Crossover Ranch. The peacocks would be screaming their heads off soon. Lovie crawled into bed with her clothes on and hugged her mother's feather pillow. *"Maybe I'm just sleep walking,"* she thought. *"If I go back to sleep again, maybe I'll wake up."* The sheer pink curtains waving gently over the open dormer window finally lulled her to sleep at midnight.

The curtains were flying horizontally over the bed, popping like wet dishtowels, the next time she opened her eyes. She sat bolt upright when she heard the wind call her name.

"L-o-o-vie. L-o-o-vie. H-e-e-re Dingo. H-e-e-re Cotton."

"Mom?" Lovie struggled out of her tangle of sheets. The comforter slithered to the floor and she slipped on it when she got out of bed. Her head reeled. She fought with the curtains that the wind seemed to be trying to smother her with. "Mom!" she yelled.

The curtains went limp. No answer came from the stillness of the courtyard below. Someone had put the alarm clock back on the bedside table. It read 2:45 A.M. FRIDAY—JUNE 23. She knocked it off again.

She could see a faint light ebbing and flowing from the chapel's stained glass window. "*Granny and Maria must have lit a lot of candles,*" she thought. She wondered if there would be any left for Angela's candlelight wedding.

She opened the bedroom door quietly and looked down the hall. Granny's door was ajar but she could not hear Grampa Hank snoring so she knew he had not come home.

Fireball bounded down the hall. She scooped him up and took him back to bed with her. He turned on his purr and happily pricked her pillow with his claws and snuggled up to her face. She blew his fur away from her nose and turned her head the other way.

"Good night, Fireball. We're sleeping-in in the morning. Nobody wants to see us anyway."

Fireball did not want to sleep-in. Two hours later the fifteen pound cat stood on Lovie's chest and dug his claws into her ribcage. He wanted out—now. She let him out into the hall but he just stood there and meowed. She picked him up, tiptoed past Granny's bedroom and went downstairs to the kitchen to feed him something to keep him quiet.

By the time she finished catering to the cat, she was wide awake. It was odd that she should be the first one to get up in the morning and not Grampa Hank. Why had he still not come home? She needed to talk to him. She needed to tell him that El Lobo robbed the Comanchero's grave; that Angela used her to lure El Lobo to the ranch to walk her down the aisle; that Granny's idea of a dream ranch was a nightmare. Most of all, she wanted her grandfather to tell her why he broke his promise to give her the ranch and to plead with him not to let Granny give it to Angela.

She decided not to wait to see if Grampa Hank was coming to the rehearsal dinner to talk to him. She pulled on her boots, buckled on a pair of chinks, grabbed a cap and hooded sweatshirt and stuffed its pockets with chocolate chip cookies that she sneaked out of a cookie jar labeled, "Pete."

The coffee pot was not set to come on for another hour. No one would wake up to hear her go as long as she did not start a vehicle. She found a flashlight in the mudroom and slipped silently onto the service porch. Fireball sneaked out ahead of her. The ostriches did not lift their heads out from under their wings.

The security light by the horse barn cast long shadows across the grass. "Here, kitty, kitty," Lovie called softly. "Walk in front of me, please. It's okay if you step on a rattlesnake. You have eight more lives. I don't know if I have any."

She was anxious to see if the horse Grampa Hank left for her yesterday was still there. She hurried down the barn alley and slid open the door, trying not to make it screech. Her answer stood alone on the back side of the lot, resting on three legs, with his head down, sound asleep.

"Brownie?" Brownie cocked an ear at her and let his air roll audibly through his nostrils. He stood up on all fours momentarily, then nonchalantly dropped his other hip and rested his other leg. Lovie haltered him and led him into the barn.

Brownie ate his grain eagerly, without drooling like he used to. His withers did not protrude as sharply as they used to either and Lovie could no longer count his ribs. He was brown again.

"Look at you, Brownie. Whatever time warp we're in seems to be agreeing with you."

Lovie's saddle was on the second saddle rack. The first saddle rack, reserved for Grampa Hank, was empty. She nudged Fireball off her saddle blanket and carried her blanket, pad and saddle to the alley. Brownie was so fat she could barely fasten the back cinch.

The eastern sky had just begun to lighten when Lovie got off Brownie to open the Horse Pasture gate. She picked a clump of small white daisies by the gate post—nice normal daisies which did not glow in the dark. The glow-in-the-dark flowers had given the headquarters an unnatural radiance that she was glad to leave behind. She pulled off the daisy petals one by one. "Dead, dreaming, dead, dreaming...."

Halfway to the river, a little band of mares and colts surrounded them. She was glad that Grampa Hank still showed a little spunk by not taking all the horses across to the River Camp as Granny mandated. But she hoped that a stud horse was not with them. A stallion will attack a gelding he thinks is competing for his mares, not that Brownie would be much competition.

The colts nipped at Brownie's mane and tail. Lovie fanned her cap at them and they raced away, kicking up their heels and roiling the fog that had settled in the low spots. Brownie showed no interest in them. "Brownie, old boy, I used the think you were a dead-head because you were old. Now I know you were a dead-head because you were a dead-head."

They found the two-track road leading to the river and Brownie plodded along, half asleep. A calf bawled in the distance—the first baby of the morning to wake up and cry for its milk. Just as the road got steeper, Brownie balked. A long thick snake lay across it. The horse pawed and switched his tail. The snake did not move. Lovie could not tell if it was a bullsnake or a rattlesnake because Brownie was giving it such a wide berth. She threw a chocolate chip cookie at it to see if it would coil up, but it did not move. Whatever kind of snake it was—it was dead.

Brownie picked up his pace on the decent to the river. Both cattle and wild hogs had left tracks on the road recently. There was also a fresh set of horse tracks. Lovie could tell that it was a shod horse with even bigger feet than Big Foot's.

At the rock crossing, Brownie sniffed at the slow-moving water then splashed in without hesitation. The runoff from the previous rain had already made its way downstream. The horse's ears perked up as he neared the bank on the opposite side. The hungry calf bawled again. This time another joined in. A cow answered and then another and another.

A hundred yards south of the river stood the red canyon wall that was visible from the chapel hill. Buzzard Point protruded from the canyon wall. Through the cottonwood trees, Lovie could just barely make out the peak of the new metal roof on the rebuilt homestead ruin. This was the homestead where the first Lovella was born and the scene of the Comanchero's demise. A mile up the river, obscured by the fog, was the River Camp. But the bawling was not coming from the River Camp. It was coming from below Buzzard Point.

Lovie clucked to Brownie to get him to speed it up. She wanted to see what was going on by Buzzard Point so she could tell Grampa Hank. She also wanted to check out the improvements to the old homestead.

Brownie sulled-up and refused to step out of the river. Lovie kicked him in the sides but all she got out of him was a hollow sounding oomph. He pawed at the water. She slapped him on the rump with the ends of her reins. He began to sidestep. He sidestepped all the way out of the river, making an arc around a large piece of driftwood. A snake had washed up with the driftwood. Its greenish-yellow belly was turned up to the sky. At one end hung a triangular head and at the other, a lifeless set of rattles. Grampa Hank used to say, "Turn a rattlesnake's belly up to the sun to make it rain." It seemed to be working.

Safely past the snake, Brownie trotted across the soft wet sand. Lovie ducked under a mesquite limb. She remembered the times Brownie had wiped her off on a low hanging limb as they made their way through the brush, trying to keep up with Grampa Hank. She allowed Brownie to follow a cow trail that seemed to be going toward the sound of the cattle. The shod horse with the big feet had followed the same trail. Then she spotted the cattle.

Too late, Lovie noticed a thin wire stretched across the trail. It crackled on contact with Brownie's legs. He made the fastest backwards move she had ever known him to make and she flipped forward, out of the saddle. She landed on her back on the sandy ground, still holding onto one rein.

She got up slowly, avoiding eye contact with the horse, so as not to appear threatening, and told him—in the sweetest voice she could muster—just how much trouble he would be in if he pulled away from her and ran off. She took a cautious step forward. Then her own leg brushed against the hot wire.

The wire snapped and sent a painful electric charge through her body. She screamed right in Brownie's face. Brownie did a one-eighty over his hocks, pulling the rein through her hand, and high-tailed it for home. At the other end of the hot wire trap, a dozen black cow-calf pairs broke through the wire and scattered. Lovie rubbed her blistered hand on her painfully tingling thigh.

Wicked laughter echoed down the canyon. From above her she heard a raspy voice, "Did Hank Moore teach you to ride like that, *pelirroja*?"

El Lobo was perched on top of Buzzard Point on a huge pale gray horse with buzzard feathers tied in its mane. The horse faded in and out of view, like a ghost horse, as fog rose out of the canyon.

Anger erased any fear Lovie might have had. "You were stealing those cattle from my Grampa Hank, weren't you, you scumbag!"

El Lobo spat a stream of tobacco juice into the fog. "Actually, I was rescuing them from your grandmother. I said to myself, 'El Lobo, why not rescue some of the stupid beasts before they eat more of those white flowers.'"

"What are you talking about?"

The pale gray horse pawed at the edge of the point, sending chunks of rock clattering to the bottom of the canyon. El Lobo brought a rawhide quirt down between the horse's ears. "Your grandmother grows poisonous flowers, and she is kind enough to make them glow in the dark so Hank Moore's cattle can poison themselves in the middle of the night if they want to. Did you not see the dead bull? How sad that the rattlesnakes are also crawling back to their dens to die."

"Rattlesnakes don't eat flowers, you stinking cattle rustler!"

"A *pelirroja* on the fight, no? It hurts El Lobo's shins to see an angry *pelirroja*. *Pelirrojas* kick like mules. I know. One kicked me once—one just like you—same frizzy red hair, same speckled face, same ugly name. Only a dumb gringo would name a girl, Lovella. When I saw you at the bull sale, I thought the first Lovella had come back to torment El Lobo. But her teeth were not all wired up like yours. You are probably a better biter—like Hank Moore's snarling white dog, no? El Lobo would have a hard time cutting the ruby cross from your neck."

"You're a sicko! You didn't steal that cross from Little Lovella. The Comanchero did. You robbed his grave to get it. Only a sicko would rob a grave. What did you do with the Comanchero's bones?"

"I shook them in front of Hank Moore's bay horse like this!" El Lobo stood up in his stirrups and flapped his arms wildly. As he did he stuck the rowels of his spurs into his own horse's sides. For a moment, Lovie feared that he and the wild-eyed ghost horse would fly off Buzzard Point. But only a buzzard feather flew to the ground.

El Lobo settled back in his saddle. "I saw you riding Hank Moore's bay horse at your mother's bull sale. That horse is *muy bravo*, no? But he is afraid of El Lobo. He threw himself over backwards to get away from me once and took Hank Moore down with him. How sad that the saddle horn smashed Hank Moore's big heart as flat as a valentine." El Lobo threw his head back and howled with laughter.

Lovie's heart dropped into the pit of her stomach. She charged the canyon wall and pounded her fists against the red rock. "So you're the reason Big Foot fell over on Grampa Hank. You're worse than a grave robber. You're a murderer!"

"Violence runs in both our families, no? But in your family it is the women who are fierce; as fierce as they are ugly. Look at this scar on El Lobo's forehead. You cannot deny that one of your women shot me right between the eyes." The ghost horse stepped nervously from side to side. "Look at my scar!"

Scar...scar...scar...echoed down the canyon. Lovie could not see El Lobo's scar—only a red glow through the fog that was now swirling around him.

El Lobo continued, "Do you know why El Lobo—The Wolf—is not carved on a tombstone in your family cemetery? Because your great-great-great-grandmother did not bother to ask me my name before she scarred me for eternity. Then your family built a fence around their cemetery and left El Lobo's grave on the outside. I had to plant flowers around my own grave—wild irises—very hardy—not poisonous."

"You're quite the comedian for a cattle-rustling murderer. You can't scare me by pretending to be the Comanchero. The Comanchero died over a hundred years ago. Now get off this ranch and quit following me around. You're nothing but a nut case and I'm not afraid of you."

"El Lobo likes a brave girl who is angry all the time. Your anger makes me stronger. I will dance with you at my Angela's wedding. Then I will take you away with me. A girl like you does not belong in your grandmother's dream world. Her dream for the Crossover Ranch is loco, no? Your dream is the one El Lobo desires. I will steal it from you. Then it will be your turn to follow me, *pelirroja*." The ghost horse's agitation earned him another whack with the quirt.

"You can't steal this ranch from me. Granny is giving it to Angela at the rehearsal dinner, for a wedding present."

"*Que triste*, how sad. It would have been more of a challenge to steal it from you. The women in my family are beautiful, but they are not so fierce. My Angela does not dream of owning a ranch. She dreams only of the green-eyed bookworm. She will hand it over to El Lobo on a silver platter."

"She'll have to borrow one from my Granny."

El Lobo's wicked laughter set Lovie's teeth on edge. "You are the comedian, *pelirroja*. *Pelirroja* is Spanish for 'redhead.' Your people speak only English. El Lobo speaks three languages. A Comanchero trader must speak English, Spanish and Comanche." El Lobo tipped his hat to Lovie, jerked on his reins and vanished into the fog that followed him out of the canyon.

Lovie decided not to give him the pleasure of hearing the words in Spanish she learned from the cowboys. "How do you say 'stinking skunk' in Spanish?" she yelled.

A lone buzzard circled Buzzard Point, then dropped over the edge and soared on the updraft, searching for its breakfast of rotted rattlesnake.

15

THE FOUNTAIN ANGEL

Lovie heard the jeep chugging down the road before she saw it. She ran from the trees to the open riverbank, plopped down on the wet sand and took off her boots and socks. She held them high and splashed across the river. The rocks on the bottom scraped her feet but did not slow her down. Whoever was driving the jeep would surely give her a ride—unless it was Angela.

Pete was driving. "Is that you, Lovie? What's up? I was test driving the jeep to see if it'd hold together and Brownie dang near ran me down. I couldn't catch him, either. He's back at the barn by now." Pete grinned and readjusted the straw hat on his red head.

Lovie grinned back, quickly covering her green and red rubber bands with her lips. "I'm fine," she said, looking down at her blistered hand. "I'd be even better if I'd let go of the reins sooner."

"What happened? Did Brownie see a snake? He hates snakes."

"Two snakes, big dead ones...." Lovie glanced back at Buzzard Point, where the sun had erased the specter of El Lobo. "...and one skunk."

Pete patted the cracked upholstery of the passenger seat. "Hop in. I'll haul you back to the barn."

"Thanks, but I need to go to the River Camp to see Grampa Hank. Is that where you're headed?"

"Mr. Hank won't be back till late this afternoon. He's shipping dry cows and picking up more candles for Angela and her mama. Those women sure can run through a box of candles."

Lovie pulled on her socks and boots and hopped into the jeep. "Do you think he has his cell phone with him? I really need to talk to him."

"We don't have any phone service right now, no cell phones, no house phones—nothing. The co-op boys told Mr. Hank there's a negative magnetic force scrambling the lines. The trouble is located somewhere on the ranch but they can't figure out what's causing it."

"Well I have more trouble to tell Grampa Hank about. There's a cattle rustler on the ranch. I found a bunch of cows and calves in a hot wire trap on the other side of the river."

"Dang. Who'd do a thing like that?"

Lovie shrugged. What Pete did not know about his future father-in-law would not hurt him, hopefully.

Pete turned the jeep around and it chugged up the road. He reached back and steadied the clumps of Granny's glow-in-the-dark flowers that were piled high in the back end.

"What are you doing with these flowers, Pete? Is Angela making you decorate your jeep for the wedding? This isn't the getaway car, is it?"

Pete grinned shyly. "No, Ma'am. I've got to take all these dang flowers somewhere and burn 'em before they go to seed all over the ranch. We had the laboratory analyze the chemical that makes 'em glow in the dark. The bad news is the blossoms are toxic to cattle and rats. The good news is they aren't toxic to birds."

"Is whatever eats the dying rat a gonner, too, Pete? Like rattlesnakes?"

"Right. That's probably what killed those two snakes you saw. The bad news is that's what killed that bull y'all found yesterday. Your Granny wanted all the cattle out of the Camposanto Pasture before the wedding, but driving 'em out woulda been a lot more fun than dragging them out. I just learned from Angela that *camposanto* means "cemetery" in Spanish."

"I just learned that *pelirroja* means redhead. I guess you'd be a *pelirrojo*."

The jeep picked up speed. The Crossover Ranch spread out around them; from Buzzard Point through the river breaks; over the pastures and winter wheat fields; up to the highest point in the county—the cross over the chapel's bell tower.

Lovie enjoyed riding in the open-topped jeep in the sunshine. She took off her cap and let the warm air blow through her hair. It felt good to a girl who had been in an ice storm two days before.

She reached into her sweatshirt pocket for a handful of cookies. They were in pieces now. "Would you like a smashed, chocolate chip cookie, Pete?"

"Sure would. Thanks. I eat these things all the time now. Angela made me give up tobacco. She said tobacco was the reason I didn't like sweets. So I figured maybe if I ate a lot of sweets, it'd make me not like tobacco. It worked. When I have a mouth full of Angela's chocolate chip cookies, it makes me sick to think of adding a lip full of tobacco."

Lovie was not surprised Angela objected to tobacco, remembering the tobacco juice that dripped out of the corner of El Lobo's sneering mouth.

They bounced over a rock outcropping where the creek crossed the road. Lovie hoped Pete noticed that the layered rock was eroding on her side. All she could see over the edge was water hitting the next tier of rocks several feet below. Instinctively, she leaned away from it, into Pete's cold arm. Pete jerked the jeep sharply away from the drop-off then overcorrected and skidded back onto the road. Lovie bounced up and down on the seat but the cookies fell through the hole in the floorboard.

Pete stole a sheepish look at Lovie. "Sorry about that."

"*El Lobo was right about one thing,*" Lovie thought. "*Pete's eyes really are green—really, really green.*"

Pete felt Lovie staring at him. His ears turned bright red. "Say, wasn't that something about the Comanchero not being in his grave?" he stammered.

Lovie did not answer. She did not have the heart to tell Pete that his evil future father-in-law thought he was the Comanchero and that he caused Big Foot to fall on Grampa Hank.

"You know, Lovie," Pete continued, "Comanchero traders didn't start out bad. They were the middlemen between the New Mexico ranchers and the Comanche Indians. The Comancheros supplied New Mexico ranchers with cattle in exchange for horses. Then they traded the horses to the Comanches for more cattle. But the Comanches were stealing the cattle from Texas ranchers who'd run the Indians off their land. Sometimes they went too far and stole their women and children, too, and held them for ransom. Eventually, the Comanchero traders figured out that if they stole from the Texans directly, they'd make more money."

"Dadgum, Pete. If you're interested in history, you should like this ranch a lot."

"I like history alright but I like science better. I like this ranch 'cause it's like a great big science lab. Your Granny is willing to let me try anything that might generate enough profit to keep the ranch afloat during drought or low cattle prices. This day and age, cattle alone can't cover the expenses of a big ranch like this."

"Do you even want to be a rancher, Pete?"

"Me? No, Ma'am. I don't believe in gambling. I really want to be a professor but once I get my Master's degree, I won't be able to afford to go on and get my Doctorate."

"Does Angela know that you don't want a ranch?"

"It's okay with her. She told me if she ever had a ranch, she'd just give it to her Papa."

"Uh...have you met Angela's Papa?"

"Not yet. She says I'll meet him at the wedding. His name is El Lobo. Awesome name, huh? It means, The Wolf."

Pete pulled the jeep up to the horse barn and turned off the key. The engine kept on shimmying. Brownie was standing in the shade of the barn, resting on three legs.

"Come over and see the fountain after you put Brownie away, Lovie. It's just about fixed. Angela's going to be real surprised when she and her mama get back from the bus station with Father Miguel."

"Who's Father Miguel?"

"Father Miguel Rios, Angela's uncle. He's going to marry us."

"Oh. Okay, thanks for the lift, Pete." Lovie was sick of talking about Angela. She wanted something to eat.

Lovie unsaddled Brownie and rinsed him off. She told him all her troubles while she scratched all his itchy spots and sprayed him for flies. He showed as much interest in her troubles as he ever had. He yawned. As soon as she took off his halter and let him go, he found a muddy spot in the pen and rolled in it. He got up looking like a corn dog.

On her way to the cookhouse to look for leftovers, Lovie saw Pete in the courtyard. He was standing on the pedestal in the middle of the fountain with one arm around the angel statue.

"Lovie, will you climb up here with me and hold these water pump pliers? I promise it'll just take a minute. I ran a new line to where it connects underneath the angel but when I turned on the water nothing happened. So I pried this panel off her back and saw that the old t-joint was corroded shut. That's why the water wasn't getting through to her hands, so I had to replace it. Just hold the perpendicular pipe steady so I can tighten the horizontal one."

Lovie climbed up beside Pete and held the pliers. She hoped he could not hear her stomach growling. He leaned against her, trying to balance on the pedestal while using both hands to tighten the pipes. "It has to be good and tight before I can turn on the water. This time I hooked up the air compressor at the other end so I can blow out the line if it's plugged up somewhere else inside her."

Pete's body was so cold it gave Lovie the shivers, but she could not get out of his way without falling into the slimy stuff that floated around in the bottom of the fountain. At the same time, Pete was becoming painfully aware of Lovie's warmth and of her wind-blown red hair that was tickling his red ears.

"Uh...Lovie," he said, in a voice that sounded like it was changing again. "Have you ever noticed how much this statue looks like Angela?"

Before Lovie had time to think of a polite answer, Angela stepped out of the cookhouse with Granny and Maria and a plump fellow in a black shirt and liturgical collar. Angela spied the two pipe fitters huddled together behind the statue. Lovie had to agree that Angela's stone face looked exactly like the statue's stone face.

Pete gave the pipes one last twist and leaped away from Lovie like she had poked him with a hot-shot. "You better jump down, Ma'am, so you don't get wet when I turn on the water."

Pete waved to his fiancée as she did an about-face to stalk back in the house. "Angela, stay there! I've got a surprise for y'all!" Then he scrambled over the courtyard wall, not an easy feat, even for a tall guy. His head popped up for one last look at Angela then ducked out of sight.

Angela sneered at Lovie and her narrowing eyes conveyed only one message: Keep away from my man!

Lovie left the fountain angel standing alone, with its palms raised to the heavens, and sauntered over to the gazebo.

"Are you ready, Angela?" Pete hollered. Angela said nothing. Pete turned on the water. Nothing happened. Not a drop of water dripped from the fountain angel's hands as promised.

"Dang!" Pete uttered. The crown of his straw hat appeared above the rock wall. "Sorry, Father. I guess one of the other pipes must be corroded. Wait one more second, y'all. I can fix her." The straw hat disappeared. The air compressor came on and chattered loudly.

Still nothing happened. Lovie started back down the steps of the gazebo.

Then it blew.

The fountain angel's plugged plumbing broke loose and decapitated her. A geyser of water shot her marble head thirty feet in the air. Everyone's eyes followed its ascent in unison. Then the marble likeness of the bride-to-be crashed to earth like a giant hail ball. It made a hole in the gazebo's new metal roof and exploded on its new concrete floor.

Lovie was thankful she was still wearing her boots and chinks as marble particles stung the bare legs of the three women standing on the porch, clinging to Father Miguel.

16

FATHER MIGUEL

After the beheading, Granny and Angela went to the greenhouse to wire and tape stems of bluebonnets and glow-in-the-dark flowers for bouquets, corsages and boutonnieres. Lovie was not invited to help. Maria went to the chapel to light candles, in case it was a bad omen to blow the head off an angel the day before a wedding.

Lovie took advantage of the empty house by slipping into her mother's short pink bathrobe and throwing her filthy dirty clothes into the washer. She threw the white towels from the clothes basket in with them. Even though her wardrobe left something to be desired, at least her clothes would be fresh and clean when Grampa Hank came to the rehearsal dinner. She was certain he would come home for that. And she was certain he would not let Granny give the ranch to Angela when she told him Angela would turn around and give it to El Lobo.

She waited upstairs for the clothes to wash and ventured downstairs just long enough to transfer the load to the dryer. Then she spent a long time in her mother's pink-tiled shower, blatantly wasting hot water, before wrapping the pink towel around her wet head and slipping back into the pink bathrobe.

The sound of singing filtered through the bathroom window. She cranked it open a few inches to see what was going on. Mariachis in matching sombreros had taken over the gazebo. Their bright sequined jackets were draped over the rails like Christmas decorations. Gleeful musicians swayed back and forth, laughing and singing. Father Miguel joined the circle with much embracing and patting on the back. He produced a small harmonica and the music started up again.

Lovie hurried downstairs in her bare feet. She separated her clothes from the load of white towels and turned the dryer back on. Her black t-shirt came out full of lint and more wrinkled than it had gone in. One side of the alien's gaunt white face was peeling off. She set up the ironing board in the mudroom and starched and ironed her jeans to make them look presentable. She sprayed starch on the alien to glue him back down but the starch just created a shiny blotch in the middle of the t-shirt.

She turned off the iron and went to the refrigerator to find something to eat besides cookies. It was stuffed with pitchers of pink lemonade and bowls full of food intended for the rehearsal dinner. She helped herself to a bowl of potato salad.

Wedged behind the potato salad was a small white book with gold tipped pages. Its blank leather cover offered no clues as to why it would be in the refrigerator of all places. It was fastened shut with a white leather strap with a gold lock. She shrugged and traded the book for a pitcher of lemonade.

She found her tall *Dallas Cowboys* mug in the cabinet of glasses by the kitchen sink and stuck it under the ice dispenser. Ice cubes dropped noisily into it.

Someone opened the mudroom door. It bumped against the ironing board, sending the iron crashing onto the tile floor. Lovie heard a man groan as he scooted the ironing board out of the way to retrieve the hot iron. "Ay-y-y-y!" he yelped as he deposited it on top of the washing machine by its cord.

Quietly, Lovie removed her mug from the ice dispenser and tied her robe tighter around her body, but the more her body was hidden, the more her legs showed. She heard the dryer door open. The towels stopped spinning. The man rummaged through them. He sounded irritated. She knew it could not be Grampa Hank. He would not have cared what color her blue jeans and black t-shirt had turned the white towels. She peeked into the mudroom.

"Father Miguel?" she said softly.

Father Miguel jumped like a guilty child. "Mary Lovella? I am looking for my white guestbook. Have you seen it?"

"Why are you looking in the dryer, Father?"

"It is my secret hiding place. My guestbook is white, like the inside of the dryer. That is why I hide it there."

Lovie was surprised he knew her name and even more surprised he was telling her where his secret hiding place was. "I think I saw it in the refrigerator," she answered.

"Why would I hide my guestbook in the refrigerator when my secret hiding place is in the dryer?" Father Miguel brushed past her, stopping to give her a puzzled look, then opened the refrigerator. "Ah, but you are right. Thank you. My guestbook is also white like the inside of the refrigerator."

"Why don't you just keep it in a bookcase?"

"Because my evil brother-in-law has been going through the bookcases, looking for it. El Lobo wants to write his name in my white guestbook, but the name, El Lobo, belongs in the black guestbook. Be a good girl, Mary Lovella. You would not like to meet the keeper of the black guestbook." Father Miguel smiled and patted Lovie on the forearm.

Before she could smile back, the cold fingers of both of his hands clamped down on her forearm. "Mary Lovella, you are still so warm!"

Lovie flung ice cubes all over the kitchen. "Let go of me!"

"I am sorry. I did not mean to frighten you. But you are much too alive to be on our side of the Crossover Ranch. You have arrived too early. You should have waited until you were old enough. Thirteen is not old enough. I should have been here when you crossed over. If I had known you were coming, I would not have let Angela talk me into taking a vacation."

Father Miguel thumbed through his guestbook. He marked a page with a gold ribbon. "I am sure your name was not in my guestbook before I left. Hmm. Something is wrong. This is not my handwriting. Your name is written in pencil. I use only gold permanent markers—*Sharpies*—fine point. Who could have written your name in my guestbook without my knowledge?"

"I bet it was Angela," Lovie snapped. She shoved her mug back under the ice dispenser and raised her voice over the clinking of ice cubes. "Angela invited me here to be in her dadgum wedding—but she doesn't really want me. She wants El Lobo. But she wasn't allowed to invite him because he's evil. He made Big Foot fall on Grampa Hank and he robbed the Comanchero's grave to get the cross he gave Maria. Actually, the freak thinks he is the Comanchero. And if he is the Comanchero, then he stole Maria's cross from Little Lovella."

As the ice cubes started to overflow, Lovie talked faster and louder. "El Lobo was following me because I was mad at Mom because Grampa

Hank promised the ranch to me but he broke his promise so Mom inherited it and she sold all the cattle and horses except Big Foot because everybody's afraid of him and to top it all off El Lobo smells like a dead skunk and he wants to dance with me at Angela's wedding because he likes angry girls and I'll be even angrier if Granny gives the ranch to Angela because she'll give it to El Lobo but the Crossover Ranch is my dream and I want it." When she had finished, the entire ice dispenser had emptied itself all over the kitchen floor.

"Could you please repeat that, Mary Lovella?"

"El Lobo is trying to steal my dream, Father!"

"El Lobo steals dreams because he has none of his own and without a dream of his own he will fall into the bottomless pit of hopelessness and cease to exist. Poof! Stay away from El Lobo, Mary Lovella, or his negativity will pull you into the pit with him. His negativity feeds on anger. More anger, more negativity, more anger, more negativity—until poof!" Father Miguel poofed right in Lovie's face. "I must go to Angela."

Lovie grabbed his sleeve. "Wait, Father. What about me? If I'm alive, that means I'm not dead, right? I'm dreaming! But it's not my dream. It's Granny's. I'm stuck in it. I want to wake up. I haven't been very nice to my mother lately and I want to tell her I'm sorry."

"Are you confessing?"

"I don't know. Am I?"

"Are you Catholic?"

"No, Father."

"Then I cannot help you. You must admit to your mother that you have hurt her and tell her you are sorry. She will forgive you because she is your mother. Then you must find a way to make it up to her."

"Then please erase my name from your guestbook and send me back to her. She only has Dingo and Cotton to protect her and Cotton is getting too old. Nobody on your side wants me for anything."

"I am a priest, Mary Lovella, not a magician. Even unwanted children are gifts from God. I cannot return a gift from God. It is not like returning something to *Walmart*." Father Miguel turned and fled down the service porch steps. One of the ostriches pecked him on his bald spot as he sped by.

"Please, Father," Lovie pleaded. "My teeth will rot if I don't get my braces off soon!"

17

THE REHEARSAL DINNER

Lovie was glad she had remembered to remove the ear tag marker from her jeans pocket before washing them. She made sure the cap was fastened tightly before sticking it back in her pocket. Its ink was black and sticky—and permanent—and certainly would have incurred Granny's wrath if it had been washed and dried with the white towels. She could not count the number of *ChapSticks* she had washed and dried and ended up with empty cylinders.

She went back upstairs to her mother's room, dressed and French braided her hair. She looked at herself in the bathroom mirror and frowned. Her hair never looked as nice as when her mother braided it for her. She twisted her maroon scrunchie around the end of her long loose braid. Maroon was about as close to pink as she cared to get. It matched her *Texas Aggie* sweatshirt.

From the window seat by the dormer window Lovie watched the comings and goings in the courtyard and waited for Grampa Hank to show up. Granny had topped the headless, marble fountain angel with a wreath of glow-in-the-dark flowers. It made her look like a valuable statue from ancient Rome. Maria and Angela set up tables on the patio and decorated them in shades of pink. When the sun disappeared behind the chapel, the sky decorated itself to match.

The mariachis moved to folding chairs by the barbecue trailer when the smoke began to smell more like barbecued brisket than mesquite wood. Either they were getting as hungry as she was, or they knew that a cloud of smoke was the best place to be at sunset when the mosquitoes came out to dine.

The buzzards had moved on after Pete disposed of the poor dead bull, but noisy blackbirds took their place as a source of irritation to all. The raucous birds increased in number throughout the afternoon and guests arriving for the rehearsal dinner took turns shooing them away from the glow-in-the-dark flowers. The blackbirds were as fond of the flowers as the big peacock that was locked in the chicken house, screaming his head off. At dusk, the blackbirds gave up the siege and flew away to roost.

Lovie heard Granny come upstairs to get ready for the rehearsal dinner but she left again without coming to talk to her. Grampa Hank had not returned to the headquarters with the new candles. She was beginning to wonder if she would ever have a chance to talk to him. Granny's dream for the ranch did not seem to include him either.

Pete came out of the bunkhouse, looking spiffy, and summoned the musicians to the rehearsal. They picked up their instruments and filed through the wrought iron gate.

The wedding party included a garishly dressed man being led around by a chubby little girl and an angelic looking little boy. Lovie assumed the newcomers were Angela's cousin and his children. They looked familiar, like someone she had seen at the little grocery store near the ranch but had not spoken to.

Father Miguel arranged the wedding party in their assigned places in the procession then he and the little boy took the lead. The entourage marched toward the thicket without Grampa Hank ever joining the parade. No one invited Lovie to follow along. She felt less popular than El Lobo. At least Angela liked him.

Pete's lighting systems came on at dusk, one by one. First came the spotlight which was pointed at the fountain. Then strings of tiny white lights began to twinkle on the gazebo and in the trees. Luminarias glowed softly along the porches and continued along the footpath to the bridge. Their light disappeared in the thicket and reappeared on the other side, guiding the procession up the hill to the chapel.

The chapel doors were closed for a long time. The chapel bell rang when the rehearsal was over and the bridal party streamed out carrying candles. They filed downhill at a lively pace and emerged from the thicket with Pete and Angela leading the way, hand in hand, with the mariachis serenading behind.

The music summoned the catering crew. They came out of the cookhouse with pitchers of iced tea and pink lemonade and plates of rolls for the tables. They lit candles of citronella-laced pink wax that had been poured into glass boots.

Each table was set with pink plates, pink napkins and pink cups. Pink baskets with pink bows served as centerpieces. The baskets were filled with bundles of *biscochitos* wrapped in pink cellophane and boxes of sparklers tied with blue ribbons. The sparklers were Pete's idea.

Pete and Angela passed by Lovie's private reviewing stand without looking up. Lovie wondered who stood in for the bride at the rehearsal since she had been demoted. Even she knew it was bad luck for the bride to stand in for herself.

Maria looked blissfully happy. Her only child was marrying a young man without a bad bone in his body. Lovie thought he was strange, but he was the good kind of strange—like her dad. Pete looked happy too. Lovie thought he should be looking worried.

Granny definitely looked worried. Grampa Hank was still not with her. She did not seem to notice her granddaughter sitting alone in the dormer window as she went around shaking hands with the men, hugging the women, and accepting compliments on how nice she looked.

It became obvious to Lovie that no one was going to take pity on her and invite her down to dinner and she was too hungry to stand there any longer feeling sorry for herself. She went downstairs as inconspicuously as she could in a glow-in-the-dark, starch-blotched t-shirt and joined the buffet line. No one spoke to her. Pete's guests probably thought she was a friend of Angela's and Angela's guests probably thought she was a friend of Pete's—from another planet.

The buffet table was laden with barbecued sausage and brisket, barbecue sauce, onions, pickles, jalapenos, pinto beans, potato salad, coleslaw, peach cobbler—pink of course—and Angela's flat rolls.

Lovie sat down at a table with the ranch hands. Even they clammed up and would not talk to her. They were too shy. They had come to help Pete with the fireworks he planned to set off following the dinner. They reminded her of Grampa Hank in their starched, white long-sleeved shirts with the top button buttoned.

They might have been too shy to talk but they were not too shy to eat. They emptied a plate of Angela's rolls, without commenting on the fact that they were hard as rocks. The ones they could not slice open, they simply buttered on top.

As everyone sat down with second helpings of barbecue, Granny climbed the steps of the gazebo and spoke into a microphone. "I want to thank everyone for coming. Maria and I have looked forward to this wedding for a long time, haven't we, Maria? It's a dream come true for both of us. Mr. Hank couldn't be with us tonight to give Pete and Angela their wedding gifts, but he sends his love."

"Oh, no," Lovie moaned. The ranch hands lifted their eyes to hers then looked back down at their food.

Granny sounded as shaky as Lovie felt. "Angela, dear, would you and Pete please come up here. Mr. Hank and I have some little surprises for you."

"Big surprises," Lovie mumbled under her breath. The ranch hands looked at each other.

Granny's boney hands clasped Angela's when Pete escorted her up to the gazebo. "This one is mostly for you, Angela dear. Pete and Mr. Hank—and as many of the ranch hands as they could bribe—have been working on this surprise for weeks."

Pete beamed. The ranch hands stopped chewing.

Granny held up a key ring. It held two keys. "This first key goes to your new ranch home. Mr. Hank and the others rebuilt my great-grandparents' homestead house at Buzzard Point for you and Pete to live in when you're at the ranch. And I want you to know this is the first project Mr. Hank has ever completed that did not involve livestock."

Giggles spread around the tables.

"But all of us realized that you might be uncomfortable in a house so close to the river. So Mr. Hank and I also want you to have the lovely old Victorian mansion in town that belonged to my grandmother, the first Lovella. She moved into it after she gave us the ranch. That fine old home made her feel secure and we hope it will bring the two of you as much peace and happiness as it brought her."

"*That was a surprise,*" Lovie thought. She stopped eating and used her pink napkin to wipe barbecue sauce off her chin. "*Do Granny and Grampa Hank intend to give Pete and Angela every asset the family ever owned?*"

Maria was crying. She hugged her soon-to-be-son-in-law who was standing there with his mouth hanging open. Angela was hugging everyone in sight. If suddenly owning an old ranch house and a mansion in town made Angela so giddy, Lovie figured she was going to pass out when Granny gave her the rest of the ranch.

Granny handed Pete a blue folder tied with a blue ribbon. "Open it, son," she prompted. "This one is mostly for you."

Lovie wanted to scream. She knew very well that blue folders like that contained deeds. Tears stung her eyes. It would be torture to have to sit and watch someone besides herself open the deed to her grandparents' ranch. If only she had been able to talk to Grampa Hank—just one more time.

Pete untied the ribbon and opened the folder. Then together, Pete and Angela unfolded the sheet of legal size paper that was inside. "Oh, Pete!" Angela squealed. Her long sleek hair glistened in the twinkling lights as she jumped up and down and clapped her hands.

That was it for Lovie. She could not watch anymore. She pushed herself away from the table, wadded up her napkin and threw it at her plate. It stuck fast to a mound of potato salad. No one noticed her stalk away. All eyes were on Angela. No one heard her slam the wrought iron gate against the courtyard wall or saw her flee down the luminaria-lit path toward the thicket.

Pete's voice was broadcast from the loud speaker perched on top of the gazebo. The sound followed Lovie as she ran.

"I'm just...well I'm...plumb honored, Ma'am," he stuttered.

Lovie let out a choked sob. "You promised the ranch to me, Grampa Hank. You promised!" Her painful outburst was drowned out by the merrymakers.

Pete stepped closer to the microphone. "I'm honored that you and Mr. Hank believe in me enough to give me this scholarship."

Lovie stopped dead in her tracks. "Scholarship?"

She wheeled around and came face to face with the pale gray ghost horse. He looked down on her with the composure of a beast that would only be afraid of the devil himself.

The horse snorted. Lovie backed up slowly. The savory smell of barbecued beef was overpowered by the putrid odor of dead skunk that assaulted her nose. In between Pete's loud tapping on the microphone, Lovie heard the jingling of spur rowels on the stone path leading to the thicket.

"Can y'all hear me?" Pete asked. "With this scholarship, I'll be able to finish my doctorate. I know my mother and daddy woulda been proud. Next to Angela, this is the best thing that ever happened to me. Thank y'all. Thank y'all very, very much!"

The cowboys whooped and lit sparklers.

El Lobo grabbed Lovie from behind. She was paralyzed by the icy chill emanating from his stinking body. Pete's sparklers sparkled in the wide steel blade of a Bowie knife that was drawing near her throat in slow motion, guided by the hand of El Lobo—the Comanchero.

Instinct told her to bring her knees up to her chest so gravity could help break her attacker's hold on her. But the leathery little man had the strength of a demon and he swung Lovie around and gave her a shake like the pop of a bullwhip. Her legs shot out in front of her then hit the earth again, jarring her teeth. He held her so tightly, she couldn't breathe.

"Do not try to trick me again, *pelirroja*." Lobo hissed into her ear. "You lied to El Lobo. You said my Angela and the green-eyed bookworm would own the Crossover Ranch tonight." He gave Lovie another furious shake. A sharp pain went through her ribcage.

In the courtyard, family and friends cheered for Pete and Angela's good fortune and Granny and Mr. Hank's generosity. Angela kissed Pete who, for once, did not shy away from the public display of affection. The happy couple had no idea that Granny had originally intended to give them the whole ranch and they did not care. The ranch was not the dream they shared.

Lovie's body heat was being sucked into the cold void that once held the Comanchero's soul. She struggled to take one last breath, certain that he was about to drain her life's blood with the point of his knife.

BANG! BANG! BANG! El Lobo froze. The guests cheered. The fireworks display had begun. High pitched whistles chased each other across the Camposanto Pasture and exploded over the thicket. BOOM! BOOM! BOOM!

Apparently the devil was not the only thing that frightened El Lobo's horse. Pete's fireworks did too. Pink, blue and silver sparks rained down over the thicket. The crazed animal reared up and pawed El Lobo between the shoulder blades.

El Lobo's knife blade nicked Lovie's neck as it was knocked out of his hand. Lovie was propelled forward onto her hands and knees. She willed her legs to move—and move fast—as one after another of Pete's colorful bombs shot glitter into the night sky.

Lovie ran toward the sounds of applause and laughter, gasping for air. She lunged at the wall and struggled to pull herself over—just ahead of El Lobo. He grabbed the back of her t-shirt, which mercifully had enough stretch left in it to allow her to gain a toehold between the layers of rock. A set of cold, bony, liver-spotted hands pulled her to safety on the courtyard side.

Her crash landing in a flowerbed of glow-in-the-dark flowers coincided with the loudest explosion of the night. The appreciative harmony of o-o-o-os coming out of the mouths of the rehearsal dinner guests masked the sound and fury of the Comanchero's cursing as he made his escape.

Granny's and Father Miguel's worried faces were the last things Lovie saw the night of the rehearsal dinner.

18

THE BRACELET

Granny's and Father Miguel's worried faces were the first things Lovie saw the morning of the wedding.

"Good morning, Lovella dear. You've come back to us." Granny patted Lovie's cold, clammy face with a soft towel and pulled another quilt up to her chin.

Lovie's heavy eyes closed again. She thought she heard Granny's voice but it faded away before she could answer. She felt Cotton's warm body snuggling beside her, trying to keep her warm, but she could not stop shivering. She felt Dingo licking her face and heard her mother calling her name but the licking stopped and the voice faded away and other voices floated in with the fog in her mind.

A loud pop came from the courtyard. A blackbird flew into the window screen and bounced back into the air. Father Miguel ran and opened the window. "Pete! Did it work?"

"Don't know yet, Father," Pete answered from below. "I'm giving it a few more pops. These dang...sorry, Father. These birds are hard to scare off. I'll try setting the timer down to three minute intervals."

Father Miguel closed the window.

Lovie's fog cleared enough so that she recognized the carvings on Granny's bedposts. She rolled her head toward Father Miguel's voice and caught a glimpse of his white collar floating somewhere between his black shirt and his featureless face.

"Is she here to stay, Miguel?" Granny asked. "Her eyes are opening a little."

"For her sake, I hope not. She is not scheduled to be our guest for years, but she is losing her body heat. If she gets as cold as we are she will be unable to cross back over to her mother on the other side. You are to blame for this, June. You destroyed Mr. Hank's will naming Mary Lovella his heir. Now she thinks Mr. Hank broke his promise and her turmoil has brought El Lobo out of his grave—again. This crawling in and out of the grave has become a nasty habit of his, although I cannot balme him in a way. Every time he leaves it vacant a family of skunks moves in. You need a dog to keep the skunks away, June."

"Miguel!"

"Anyway, El Lobo continues to seek retribution against your family for his demise. He tried to punish you through Maria and now he has used Angela against Mary Lovella."

"I didn't mean to put Lovella in danger. I just didn't want her to keep Hank's dream alive. I thought it would jeopardize my dream of running the ranch my own way. Hank ran it his way since the day we were married. But my grandmother gave the ranch to me, too. It didn't occur to me that the ranch would be ruined if Elizabeth had to sell so much of it to pay estate taxes or that eventually Lovella would have to pay them again if anything was left."

"Let me see if I understand running the ranch your way. You destroyed Mr. Hank's will and you invented poisonous flowers. Now both sides of the Crossover Ranch are in disarray."

"I didn't mean to make them poisonous. I meant to make them beautiful for Angela. I hoped that a beautiful wedding would help make up for what happened to her when she was a little girl—and to Maria."

"Maria has herself to blame for what happened. She froze in the middle of the river from guilt, because she was helping her husband commit a crime. She failed to protect her own child because she was too weak to stand up to El Lobo's evil. Now his evil is feeding on Mary Lovella's anger—anger that you caused. You must forgive Mr. Hank for firing that gunshot and let him move back to the headquarters. You have to share your dreams for the ranch. Shared dreams are powerful. You kept Mr. Hank from sharing his dream with Mary Lovella. Your dream does not even include her. How do you expect her to survive in a dream that does not include her?"

POP! A cloud of blackbirds covered the window and cast a shadow over Lovie's pale face. She shuddered and mumbled something unintelligible. Granny nudged Father Miguel over to the window and lowered her voice.

"Will you stop lecturing me, Miguel? I have forgiven Hank and he has forgiven me. I told him I was sorry for my selfishness and asked him to sign a new will placing the ranch in trust for Lovella. He backdated it and had it witnessed and notarized by former employees of the ranch who have also crossed over."

"Is that legal, June?"

"They say that dead people vote in Texas all the time. Why can't they sign wills?"

"Good point. If you like, I will hide Mr. Hank's new will in my secret hiding place and seal it with duct tape. Mary Lovella knows where my secret hiding place is."

"You have a secret hiding place? Where is it?"

"In the dryer. Who would think to look there?"

"Why the dryer? Why not the vault?"

"You have a vault?"

Pete's popper popped and birds squawked. Lovie rubbed her eyes and squinted in the daylight. "Granny? Is it morning? Why am I in your bed?" She wiped her hair out of her face and discovered the bandage on her neck. "El Lobo pulled a knife on me last night."

"I know, Lovella dear. I saw him."

Lovie sat up slowly. "It was a Bowie knife, Granny. El Lobo and the Comanchero are the same guy."

"I know, dear."

"I know, too, Mary Lovella," Father Miguel chimed in. "I saw him chasing you. I threw a cherry bomb at him. Pete gave them to me when he was setting up fireworks for the rehearsal dinner. I still have some." He produced a handful. Granny glared at him and the cherry bombs went back into his pocket.

The popper popped again and Father Miguel gasped. "Look at all those blackbirds! I do not like to see so many blackbirds on Angela's wedding day. Maria will think they are a bad omen. Where did Pete get that popper thing, June?"

"From a watermelon farmer in East Texas. He used it to frighten the deer away."

"Maybe the popping will keep El Lobo away. His time in the grave with the skunks has given him a rather unpleasant odor, has it not? His body is corrupt because his soul is corrupt."

Granny signaled him to lock his mouth and throw away the key.

"You need to rest now, Lovella dear," she said. "Lie back down under the covers and try to get warm. Maria and I will be downstairs in the dining room if you need us. The neighbor ladies have been bringing wedding cakes all morning."

Lovie could not rest with all of Pete's popping. Her neck hurt. Her ribs hurt. And she couldn't shake the chill that had penetrated the rest of her bones. She dragged a blanket to Granny's window seat and watched with amusement the army of blackbirds occupying the courtyard. Pete was alternating popping with rock chunking. Apparently, he did not feel that blackbirds warranted a place in the ecosystem.

Lovie heard Granny and Maria laughing with the other ladies downstairs. Since the blanket was not warming her anyway, she left it on the window seat and went downstairs in her wrinkled clothes to see what was going on. The ladies were arranging their decorated cakes on silver trays like entrants in an upscale county fair.

"Good morning, Mary Lovella!" Maria sang. "Would you like a piece of cake, m'ija? The ladies will give you the choice of any color you want as long as it is pink."

For once, Lovie was not hungry. "No thank you. Maybe a little later. Save me that piece with the little bride and groom on it."

All the ladies giggled—even Granny. "Come with me to the study, Lovella. I have something for you to give Angela."

"Angela is in the cookhouse hiding from Pete, m'ija," Maria added. "It is bad luck for the bride and groom to see each other before the wedding."

Lovie followed Granny to the study and was handed a small velvet box. "I'd like you to give this to Angela for her *something new*. This is her wedding day, a day to be happy—not angry. I know the two of you haven't gotten along and I thought this might help you clear the air."

Lovie pried open the lid of Angela's velvet box. Inside was a pair of brilliant, round-cut diamond earrings, set in circles of white gold. "Granny, these match the tennis bracelet Dad gave Mom for Christmas!"

"Your father has very good taste. He's a good man, Lovella. It's time I admitted it. I bought these with your mother in mind but I never had the chance to give them to her. Right now Angela needs them more. Her father is not a good man. It would be a gesture of friendship for you to give them to her."

"She doesn't want me for a friend."

"Try, Lovella. Please try."

The blackbirds were making a big mess in the courtyard. The popper from the watermelon patch was not discouraging them in the least. When Lovie got to the fountain, she saw that there was nothing left of the wreath around the headless angel's neck but stems.

Pete hollered from outside the courtyard wall, "Lovie, stay where you are! I'm turning on the water!" Lovie ducked.

Water began to trickle from the angel's hands.

"Pete! You fixed her!"

Pete climbed back over the wall and washed his hands in the new stream of water. "It was easy. I pretty much got the pipes cleaned out yesterday. Uh...Lovie, I've been wanting to ask you something. Can I have a lock of your hair?"

Wherever this was leading, Lovie was pretty sure it would not further her friendship with Angela. "What for?"

"I want to look at it under the microscope, to compare it to Angela's. Her hair is real straight and silky, but I've never seen hair as fine and kinky as yours. I want to see what makes it that way."

Lovie picked up a rock and hurled it at a bunch of blackbirds and went on her way without uttering Grampa Hank's off-color words that were on the tip of her tongue.

"Lovie? Wait up. I took the pups to the River Camp but they won't quit crying and they won't eat. So I brought 'em back to Angela, but her mama won't let me see her. She thinks it's bad luck for the groom to see the bride before the wedding. Will you sneak 'em in to her?"

"Sure, Pete, no problem. Angela is in the cookhouse. Meet me in the breezeway with the puppies in a little bit. I'll tell her not to come out."

Angela was sitting at the long dining hall table, arranging a mountain of wedding gifts.

"Hi, Angela," Lovie said cheerfully. "Do you need any help opening them?"

Angela looked at her coldly.

"Just kidding. Here's another one." Lovie held out the velvet box. "Sorry this one isn't wrapped, but you need to open it now anyway. It's your *something new*."

Angela did not seem comfortable with Lovie's sudden generosity.

"Really, Angela, open it. You'll like it."

Angela stroked the velvet lid before opening it. Her eyes widened when she saw the diamond earrings. "Lovie! Thank you! These earrings are beautiful! They match the bracelet Papa gave me." Angela held out her dainty wrist. It was encircled in matching round-cut diamonds, set in round white-gold links. "Papa said not to show it to you, but I want to prove to you how thoughtful he is."

"That's my mother's new tennis bracelet! Dad gave it to her for Christmas." Lovie reached for the bracelet.

Angela jerked her wrist away. "No! Papa gave me this bracelet!"

"Your Papa stole it from my mother. I can prove it. Take it off and read the clasp."

Angela's lip quivered. "It says, 'EMG'. Is that the brand name?"

"It's my mother's initials. Elizabeth Moore Grady." Lovie stuck out her hand. "So give it back. Your Papa is a dadgum thief."

"Yours is an orthodontist!" Angela fired back.

"What's that got to do with anything? Do you even know what an orthodontist is?"

"Papa told me it's someone who charges too much money for something that's a waste of money in the first place."

"That's easy for you to say. You were born with straight teeth."

Angela flashed her naturally perfect smile at Lovie then dismissed her by scooting her chair up close to the table with her back toward her. She tossed her long, silky black hair triumphantly. It cascaded down the back of the chair.

Lovie was fed up with Angela's attacks on her mother. Perhaps Angela had a right to be mad at her mother about the dirty trick she played on Maria. Perhaps Angela had a right to alter her mother's wedding gown and wear it without her permission. But Lovie drew the line in the sand—as Col. Travis had done at the Alamo—about Angela keeping the Christmas present her mother had received from her father.

Lovie slowly and deliberately took the ear tag marker out of her pocket, quietly popped off the cap and clenched the marker in her teeth. Then with all the strength she could muster, she snatched big hanks of Angela's hair with both hands and smacked her head against the back of her chair.

"Ouch!" Angela screamed, reaching in vain for Lovie's hands. Lovie pinned Angela's chair against the table with her knee and pulled her hair for all she was worth. It had the same effect on Angela as a nose twitch on a horse. Angela stopped fighting and sat very still.

"Listen up," Lovie sputtered. "I have an ear tag marker in my mouth and if you don't give me back my mother's bracelet, I'm gonna write my name on your forehead, so big your mother's mantilla won't cover it. Grampa Hank has cows with ear tags I made him when I was in the third grade. You can still read them. So what'll it be?"

Angela took off the bracelet and slammed it on the table.

Lovie snatched it up and ran. "And don't come outside!"

She met Pete in the breezeway, pulling a red wagon up the steps with the cardboard box of puppies wedged in it. Angela burst outside and hurled the earring box at Lovie as hard as she could hurl it. It exploded against her shoulder and a glimmer of earrings fell through the cracks in the plank floor.

Angela shrieked when she saw Pete. She ran back inside and slammed the kitchen door. Pete just stood there with a dumb look on his face. The bravest puppy peeked over the edge of the box to see what the fuss was about.

Lovie popped the cap back on the ear tag marker and dropped it in her pocket along with her mother's bracelet. "Well, Pete," she said, "I guess that's why the groom isn't supposed to see the bride before the wedding."

19

THE WEDDING

"So much for making friends with Angela," Lovie said. She unloaded boxes of flower arrangements from Granny's *Cadillac* and used them to prop open the chapel doors.

Granny unloaded a box of wreaths. "Tell her you're sorry, Lovella. Sometimes it helps to say you're sorry even when you're not. That way, at least one of you isn't angry anymore."

Lovie helped Granny hang glow-in-the-dark wreaths on the chapel doors. Pete made a new bell pull by braiding catch ropes together. He did not have time to install it inside where it belonged so he left it hanging temporarily down the outside of the bell tower. Granny tied a large pink bow to the knotted end.

They arranged baskets of long-stemmed pink bluebonnets on one side of the chapel and blue bluebonnets on the other side and draped the rafters with fragrant glow-in-the-dark garlands. Lovie set new kindling in the corner fireplace in case the night was colder than expected. Grampa Hank must have come through with more candles when Lovie was not looking because Granny was able to replace all the burned ones in the horseshoe candelabras and votive cups at the foot Saint Francis' stained glass window. Pete rigged up a solar spotlight on the outside so Saint Francis and his birds and beasts could be seen from the inside after dark. Lovie had to admit that all-in-all it was a perfect lighting scheme for a building without electricity.

Granny's flowers were unusually fragrant in the confines of the chapel. The scent was delightful at first, but became oppressive as the afternoon wore on and Lovie was teary-eyed by the time they finished decorating. They loaded empty boxes back into the *Cadillac* and headed to the house through the growing flock of blackbirds. The birds took to the air as they drove by, only to settle back down on treetops, rooftops and power lines.

"Take the rest of the bows to the horse barn, will you, Lovella? The draft horses should be there by now and Angela wants bows tied to the harnesses. It's nearly five o'clock. The wedding starts at seven. I'm going upstairs to get ready."

Lovie did not want to spoil the pleasant hours she had just spent with Granny by asking, "What about me?" As she carried the box of bows to the barn a pair of blackbirds dive-bombed her head. Pete was wrong about Granny's flowers not being toxic to birds. Even though the flowers were not killing them, they were making them drunk.

The horse barn was a flurry of activity as teams of horses were washed and brushed and braided. The chubby little girl Lovie had seen the night before met her at the barn door.

"Oh look! Your bows are so big!" she said. "Everything is big here. I never saw such big horses. I want to ride one so I can look in the windows of that big house. I never saw such a big house in my whole life. Daddy won't let me go inside, but it's okay if I look in the windows, huh? I'm a flower girl. Daddy's cousin is getting married. She's real pretty and her name is Angela. Angela sounds like angel. My name is Gabriela but Daddy calls me Gabby. Why do you have a bandage on your neck? Did you get that bandage at Daddy's grocery store. Daddy's grocery store has everything. Do you live here? What's your name?"

Lovie took a deep breath. One of them needed to. "My name is Lovie."

"Lovie sounds like love. Love and Angel. You must be best friends. My flower girl dress is pink and I'm not allowed to touch the lace with dirty hands. A queen wore it once. My *Tia* Maria made it small for me but it itches and Angel's shoes hurt my toes. It's okay if I take them off when no one's looking, huh?" Gabby giggled and the corners of her mouth disappeared into her round face.

She gestured for Lovie to lean closer. "Love," she whispered, "I saw the secret puppies in the house next to *Tia* Maria's, the one with all the bunk beds. They were crying. I think they were scared of that buffalo with his head stuck through the wall."

Lovie laughed. "So that's where Granny stashed Grampa Hank's buffalo head."

A male voice called anxiously for Gabby. Lovie pointed to him and said, "Look over there, Gabby; I think your daddy wants you to go put on your pretty pink dress for the wedding."

"Can you come, too, Love? I want to show you the puppies."

"I'll come later. Angela is real busy right now and I don't want to bother her."

The little girl ran wildly across the road toward her father. At the last second, she dodged his open arms, detoured by the ostriches and darted up the service porch steps into the main house. Granny would soon meet Gabby, giving herself a tour of the "big house."

The ranch hands were busy parking cars and pickups near the arena where the guests were to meet the wagons that would shuttle them up to the chapel. As each team of horses pulled away from the barn, straps of silver bells on their harnesses jingled softly. It reminded Lovie of the sound of sleet slipping off the metal roofs the last night she saw her mother—or of spur rowels against a stone path. But she did not want to think about anything connected to El Lobo.

Lovie stayed in the barn for awhile, petting a purring Fireball and feeling like Cinderella. She had no fancy clothes to wear to a party she was no longer invited to and she missed her mother. Her heart also ached for Grampa Hank. She thought surely he would have come home to dress for the wedding. But as far as she knew, he had not. She picked up Fireball, her only friend, and lugged him to the gazebo to watch everyone else have a good time.

Father Miguel appeared on the cookhouse porch a little before seven and was welcomed by the merry wedding party assembling around the fountain. The blackbirds had gone to bed but a thunderhead was waking up behind the chapel hill. The temperature dropped ten degrees while everyone found their places in the procession. The mariachis gladly donned their sequined jackets and readied their instruments. They marched slowly and respectfully, two by two, down the narrow path to the chapel. Their music was muted by the thick foliage of the trees in the thicket.

Lovie shivered. She wished she had run upstairs for her sweatshirt before ensconcing herself in the gazebo. The big cold cat in her lap was not helping and the longer she sat there the colder she became.

Gabby's little brother was Father Miguel's crucifer, his cross bearer. He looked like a cherub in his flowing white tunic. He struggled, with as much dignity as he could muster, to keep the tall, hand-carved cross from tipping sideways.

Gabby came out of the cookhouse, wearing the altered pink prom dress and carrying a puppy. Her father followed along behind in a yellow plaid jacket, swinging a basket of flower petals. "Please, *m'ija*," he begged. "Put the puppy down and carry your basket. Puppies aren't allowed in the chapel."

"Yes they are, Daddy. Angel told me that's where they used to live, and this puppy wants to go back there—right now."

"Gabby. Put the puppy down."

"No."

"Gabby!"

"No!"

Granny walked briskly down the porch of the main house, like the Queen Mother. She wore a turquoise silk dress and matching shoes. Her silver hair was tucked into a loose bun that made her curly tendrils look like they were let loose on purpose. A corsage of tiny white blossoms was pinned to her collar and a lace handkerchief was tucked into her sleeve to guard against either an attack of emotion or an allergic reaction to the glow-in-the-dark flowers, whichever came first.

One of Lovie's table companions from the night before came out of the bunkhouse wearing a tuxedo jacket with the pant legs of his starched blue jeans tucked into his tall, red-topped boots. He was pulling the wagonload of puppies. The puppy Gabby clutched to her heart began to whimper for its littermates.

The tuxedoed cowboy spotted Lovie and pulled the wagon over to her. Fireball took one look at the pups, dug his claws into Lovie's legs and bailed off her lap. "I wouldn't ask you this if I wasn't in a pickle, Ma'am, but would you mind takin' care of these pups? I had a heck of a time roundin' 'em all up and they won't quit whinin'. Pete didn't have time to feed 'em their milk and I gotta go be his best man."

Lovie rubbed her punctured legs and nodded. The fellow smiled shyly and bounded over to open the gate for Granny. He offered her his arm like it was the most natural thing in the world and escorted her soberly down the path to the chapel. Then he ran back down the hill to Pete who was hiding outside the courtyard wall so Angela would not see him again until he fell into the procession behind Father Miguel.

Angela stepped out of the cookhouse. She had chosen to wear the wedding gown over a full hoop skirt and it took up most of the breezeway. Maria hovered around it, arranging her mantilla over the gown's long satin train. Maria had graciously stepped into Lovie's place as honor attendant. She now had the dual role of matron of honor and mother of the bride. Angela nervously scanned the faces of all the players in her private drama. When she saw Lovie, she shielded the ruby cross with a gloved hand.

The beautiful bride's worried expression made Lovie feel sorry for having thrown such a fit about the cross. Although she reached into her pocket to make sure her mother's bracelet was still safely in her possession, she was resigned to the fact that the ruby cross had now been passed from one generation to the next in Angela's family. It had become Angela's family heirloom. Somehow Lovie knew that the first Lovella would be at peace with her cross being in Angela's hands. Lovie mouthed a silent, *"I'm sorry,"* to Angela—and meant it. Angela believed her and mouthed a silent, *"Me, too,"* in return.

Gabby's little brother led the wedding procession. Father Miguel followed closely behind, looking very dignified, his official duties having begun. He had vested as though he would be blessing a marriage in a cathedral instead of a small family chapel. His white brocade chasuble swayed grandly over the luminarias that were used every Christmas at the ranch to light the path of the Christ Child.

Pete joined the procession behind his best man. He walked alone, having no mother or father to escort him. Lovie thought that might have been a good job for Grampa Hank but he was nowhere to be seen. Pete was afraid to even sneak a peek at Angela for fear of starting off on the wrong foot with his new mother in law. He would see her soon enough when he took his place in the chapel and turned to watch her cross the threshold.

Gabby's frantic father implored her to put the puppy back in the box and carry the flower basket. She refused again with a squeal that echoed over the creek.

"It is alright *m'ijita*," Maria said kindly. "Take the pretty puppy with you but please go. It is your turn. Angela cannot go until you do."

That was the instruction Gabby was waiting for. She stuck out her chin and held the pup tightly to the lace bodice of her dress and passed haughtily through the courtyard gate. The glow-in-the-dark halo on her head shone through the dusky light, which was dimming quickly because of the emerging storm clouds. Lovie hoped the wind would not pick up, or Gabby's sleeves might inflate and carry her away.

Maria glowed from the inside as she picked her way toward the bridge. She tried not to soil her pink satin shoes, so that they would continue to match her pink satin suit. She handed Angela a pink *Kleenex* when the bride was overcome by a sneezing fit from the blossoms of her bridal bouquet.

Angela paused every few steps for her mother to detach her train from some obstacle or other. Every time she stopped, she looked around in vain for the father who had promised to walk her down the aisle. Lovie knew what broken promises felt like and she was genuinely sorry for Angela. At the same time, she was happy for her, and for Maria, that the evil El Lobo was nowhere to be seen—or smelled.

Maria whispered something in Gabby's father's ear and he chivalrously offered his yellow plaid clad arm to the beautiful princess that Angela was. Satisfied with this arrangement, the bride continued her forward progress.

Lovie stood by the gate and watched them go. Her wagonload of puppies clambered to peek out of their cardboard box. They began to yelp when the last of the procession entered the thicket. So did the one in the flower girl's arms. The procession came to another standstill.

Angela experienced a moment of panic. She looked desperately back to Lovie for help. Lovie immediately pulled the wagon through the gate and down the path after them, endeavoring to keep the puppies within sniffing distance of each other and out of Granny's sight at the same time. Angela smiled. Lovie smiled back and for a brief moment she felt a little warmth creeping back into her body.

The little crucifer was stopped at the bridge by the heavy cross he labored to carry. It hung up on the bridge's handrails because it would not fit through sideways. Father Miguel carried it across for him. Angela kept gliding along, tall and regal, while Maria kept her lace mantilla safe from any mesquite branch that might reach out to snare it in a sudden gust of wind.

The windmill behind Lovie creaked and started to turn. Wind gusts whistled through the treetops above her, obscuring the clomping of the draft horses as they made their way up the road with the last wagonload of wedding guests. The brewing storm was moving closer.

The crucifer proudly readjusted his cross into its upright position. The unwieldy cross did not catch in the wind as Lovie expected it to. No one in the procession seemed bothered by the wind anymore—but her. After the last of the entourage was well up the hill, Lovie crossed the bridge. The creek was more riled up than usual. She felt its energy through the planks under her feet. After she and her wagonload of panting puppies made it across, she breathed a sigh of relief that El Lobo had not grabbed her ankle like an ugly troll.

The procession was greeted at the chapel with music from the mariachis' violins. Granny was seated on the front row, on the bride's side. Grampa Hank's space was the only unoccupied seat in the house. Everyone inside stood up as Father Miguel entered the chapel behind his crucifer and processed to the front. The best man led the bridegroom to his place by the altar rail and they turned to greet the bride. Lovie wished she were in a better position to see the look on Pete's face when he was finally able to see Angela.

After the groom, the next thing everyone saw was a flower girl carrying a puppy down the aisle. Pete stole a sheepish look at Granny. When Gabby neared the altar rail, she calmly stepped out of her uncomfortable shoes and veered over to the stained glass window of St. Francis to show his birds and lambs to her puppy. Maria, just as calmly, scooted the shoes aside as she passed.

The mariachis sounded their trumpets. Gabby's father led Angela gently into the chapel then sent her down the aisle alone so as not to detract from her glory. He and Angela's full dress would not have fit between the benches at the same time anyway. He remained near the open door, holding the basket of petals and praying that his little flower girl and her puppy would not do anything else to embarrass him. Even without a wagonload of canines in tow, Lovie would not have been able to enter the chapel. There was no room to stand.

Tears streamed from the wedding guests' eyes, not so much from the tender moment as from the glow-in-the dark flowers which were making them wheeze and sneeze. Angela's eyes were fixed on those of her groom—and his were fixed on hers. The nearer she came, the deeper his dimples sank in. The best man held onto Pete's elbow to keep him from meeting his bride halfway down the aisle. The lightning zigzagging through the clouds outside was nothing compared to the electricity present inside the chapel.

Lightning struck the cemetery.

The clap of thunder was heard by every creature on the ranch with ears to hear. The bride turned whiter than her wedding gown. She leapt into the groom's arms before Father Miguel could even say, "In the name of the Father..."

Gabby's father tiptoed to the doorway to look outside. He stood there trying to decide which was worse—a mass allergy attack or projectile rainwater. He seemed not to notice Lovie standing four feet in front of his face.

Thunder rumbled, long and low. It felt as though it were coming from underground, rather than from the sky. Lovie hoped the vibration would not damage the old rock chapel's foundation. The chapel bell began to toll erratically. The hair on the back of her neck stood up. She looked up and saw El Lobo shinnying down the bell pull.

20

GRAMPA HANK

El Lobo let go of the bell pull and dropped to his feet in front of Lovie and the pups, blocking their entry into the chapel. The wind swirled around and around him, sending raindrops flying every which way.

"Granny!" Lovie screamed at the top of her lungs.

No one inside the chapel turned around.

Father Miguel said, "Hear our prayers for Pete and Angela." Pete and Angela bowed their heads. Pete winked at Angela. Angela nudged him with her elbow.

"Granny! Help me!"

Gabby's father stepped into the open threshold and looked up at the sky. He stuck out his hand to check for raindrops. Lovie watched in horror as his yellow plaid sleeve passed right through El Lobo's scrawny chest. Neither of them flinched.

Satisfied that it had indeed started to rain, Gabby's father pulled his arm back into the chapel and quietly closed the doors. He was unaware of the evil demon keeping Lovie from entering the chapel. El Lobo was not his demon.

El Lobo's wicked laughter made the puppies whimper and squeeze closer together in the bottom of the box. The scar between his eyes glowed an angry red as he raised his Bowie knife into the striking position. Lovie felt as if she were being drawn into the vortex of El Lobo's negative magnetism. The box of puppies levitated out of the wagon.

Suddenly the rope bell pull coiled around El Lobo like a snake. He cursed and slashed at it like a wild animal. Lovie was released. She snatched the cardboard box out of the air, slammed it back into the wagon and hauled it down the hill as fast as she could go without tipping it over. The fluffy white pups bounced around like popcorn.

Lightning struck the path behind her.

She heard the draft horses running down the road to escape the lightning that seemed to be chasing her—or chasing El Lobo—who was chasing her. There was nothing but darkness ahead, no luminarias, no twinkling white lights. The sound of sleet splashing into the creek led her to the bridge. Thorny mesquite branches slapped at her face and neck and ripped off her bandage.

The narrow wooden bridge was already slushy. The wagon jackknifed between the handrails and sent Lovie skidding across, flapping her arms to keep from slipping into the surging water. The puppies spilled onto the bridge. Before Lovie could regain her footing enough to gather up the pups, El Lobo caught up to them. The demon booted the helpless little creatures out of his way to get at Lovie. They cried out in pain.

From the other side of the bridge, Cotton lunged out of the darkness with her teeth bared. The giant white dog body-slammed the demon onto the bridge. As El Lobo's stinking breath was knocked out, the wind died down.

Cotton stood guard over him, snarling and drooling on his scarred face. The puppies whined excitedly and wobbled across El Lobo's legs to get a closer look at their mother. She snatched up the bravest one by the scruff of his neck and carried him up the hill to safety. The rest wobbled happily behind. They huddled underneath her belly when she stopped to look back at Lovie.

"Good girl, Cotton! Good girl!" Lovie did not want to crawl over the demon as the pups had done. She watched as Cotton sniffed the six little fluff balls. She licked them on their muzzles and under their tails and herded them up the hill in search of number seven.

Lovie tried to figure out how to get around El Lobo's prone body without touching him. She did not want to return to the wedding smelling like a dead skunk. She thought about backing up for a running start and a long jump but El Lobo raised a scrawny arm and clamped his fingers around a handrail.

With an angry groan, he pulled himself up and stood reeling on the bridge, waving his knife over his head. The wind began to howl around him again and El Lobo, The Wolf, howled with it.

"Grampa Hank! Where are you! I'm afraid!"

Just as terror gripped her heart, large cold hands gripped her shoulders and backed her off the bridge. Grampa Hank whispered in her ear. "You're not afraid, are you, Lovella?"

"Grampa Hank?"

But Lovie was afraid—afraid to turn around; afraid Grampa Hank was not really there; afraid she might not be able to resist the pull of El Lobo's evil. She could not think. She just blurted out the response Grampa Hank had drilled into her head since childhood. "No, Sir, Grampa Hank! I'm not afraid of anything!"

He made her say it when she saw her first stinging scorpion, her first rattlesnake, her first wildfire. He made her say it the first time she got bucked off; the first time she got flattened by a mama cow; the first time she rode into a crowding pen full of bulls bigger than her horse.

From somewhere deep inside Mary Lovella Grady came, "I'm not afraid of you, El Lobo. You're trespassing. The Crossover Ranch is my dream and you're not in it. I won't let you steal it away from me—ever!"

"That's my girl, Lovella. Give him hell!"

Lovie opened her mouth to give El Lobo the tongue lashing of his miserable life, but he collapsed back onto the bridge before she had time to spit out the words. Like the eye of a hurricane, an eerie stillness filled the thicket. Then the bridge shivered and splintered and collapsed into the creek. Icy water rushed over El Lobo's contorted face. Lovie took a step toward him.

"No, Lovella!" Grampa Hank ordered. It was the first time she had ever heard fear in his voice. He wrapped his strong arms around her.

A sinkhole opened up beneath the broken bridge and sucked it under, taking El Lobo with it. The demon shrieked and reached out to her. Lovie watched him fall deeper and deeper and deeper into the bottomless pit of hopelessness where the keeper of the black guestbook resided.

She squeezed her eyes shut and covered her ears. "Please don't let me go, Grampa Hank. I have to see Mom again. I have to tell her I'm sorry I got so mad at her. I'm sorry I used your cusswords. I'm sorry I rode Big Foot when I wasn't supposed to. I'm sorry I pulled Angela's hair. I'm sorry…"

A geyser of fire shot up through the hole. The heat scorched Lovie's face and the leaves on all the trees in the thicket curled up and blew off. Grampa Hank swung her away from the inferno just as the fire was met by a bolt of lightning that forced it back where it came from and sealed the hole. Steam was all that rose from the site.

The chapel bell began to ring. The happy people at the top of the hill heard the joyous sound of wedding bells for the new Mr. and Mrs. Peter Duncan Upchurch, Jr. The two people standing at the bottom heard it ring a death knell for the Comanchero.

The warm steam rising silently from the creek was quickly turning into cold fog. Grampa Hank let go of Lovie. "What's that you said about pullin' Angela's hair?"

Lovie looked down at the fog creeping up around her legs. "I promise I won't do it again. I've been looking all over the place for you, Grampa Hank. Where were you?" She looked up and he was gone. "Grampa Hank! Where are you?"

"I'm up here, Lovella. I'll always be here somewhere. I poured my heart and soul into this ranch." Lovie followed the sound of his voice up the hill and found him leaning against the windmill tower, wearing his silver belly hat and long yellow riding-slicker. "I checked on your mother for you. Just so you know—it isn't her fault the ranch is in such a mess. It's Granny's and mine. We never saw eye-to-eye on a dadgum thing. But I guess you can teach old dogs new tricks 'cause we finally learned that it's a good thing to follow our dreams as long as our dreams don't ruin somebody else's. We learned it from seein' the trouble we caused you, Lovella."

He held out her *Texas Aggie* sweatshirt and down vest. "Granny sent these for you to put on. It's too cold out here to be runnin' around in a t-shirt." He tilted his head for a better look at the alien on the front. "Don't people believe in the strangest things?"

She gladly pulled the sweatshirt over her head and snapped up the vest. "What are you gonna do now, Grampa Hank? Are you going to the reception?"

"Not till I mend one more bridge." Even if the bridge had still been there, they could not have seen it through the thickening layer of fog. "The Crossover Ranch is yours now, Lovella. A promise is a promise. But let your mother and daddy help you till you're old enough to run it on your own. Thirteen is not old enough. And don't be too bull-headed to try somethin' new once in a while either. I wish I had. And quit bein' angry all the time. You don't need to go invitin' trouble. Every time El Lobo shows up on this outfit, there's the devil to pay."

Grampa Hank unsnapped his slicker and took a folded sheet of paper out of his shirt pocket. "Here's the registration certificate on that bull you found in the creek. Use him to rebuild your herd."

"But he's dead."

"He's not dead. Didn't you hear him bellerin' in the thicket where your cows were bedded down?"

"But Mom sold those cows to a ranch in Mexico." Lovie's teeth chattered so hard she could barely form her words.

"The deal's off. The politicos on both sides of the border are squabblin' and they closed the port of entry till they get it all ironed out. No cattle are allowed in or out." Grampa Hank took off his hat, frowned at the muddy dog prints all over it and pressed it down on Lovie's head till her ears stuck out. Then he held out his yellow slicker for her to put her arms into. "Get somebody to take care of Big Foot for me, Lovella. The old boy didn't mean to hurt me. And take Dingo with you to Santa Fe when you go back to school. He can't stay at the ranch by himself. Your daddy's a good man. He'll learn to like the little dog."

The dense fog rising up between them was turning into freezing mist. Lovie hoped it kept Grampa Hank from seeing the tears forming in her eyes. She sniffed and wiped her nose with the slicker's vinyl sleeve. "What about Cotton, Grampa Hank?"

"Cotton crossed over the bridge. She needs to stay on our side with her pups. It's okay with Granny. Cotton and her pups can help us dig up all those dadgum poison flowers." Grampa Hank waved away the mist with his big hands. "One more thing. I moved your saddle up to the first saddle rack. You're the boss now."

Lovie could no longer hold back her tears. Grampa Hank pulled her close and held her tight. She felt his heart beating. He smelled like the same aftershave he had used since she was a little girl. His voice softened. "It's up to you now to keep the wolf away from the door. You aren't afraid are you, Lovella?"

"I'm not afraid of anything, Grampa Hank. Just don't let go, okay." Even though she was hugging him as hard as she could, she knew she could not keep him from slipping away.

"So long, Lovella," he whispered. "I hear your mother callin' you."

Lovie could not hear anything. She could not see anything and she could not breathe. She collapsed onto the frozen ground.

Something sank its teeth into the heel of her boot.

21

MOM

"Lovie! Lo-o-o-vie!"

Lovie thought she heard her mother calling her name. She thought she felt the frozen hard ground where she had fallen. The world was spinning around. Maria and Angela had fallen into the river...Big Foot had fallen on Grampa Hank...Pete's jeep had fallen into the Comanchero's grave...El Lobo had fallen...and fallen...and fallen...

Dingo let go of Lovie's boot heel. He ran to her face and licked her nose and mouth and eyelids with his warm slimy tongue. She gasped for air and tried to push him away. He snared Grampa Hank's hat and scampered off with it.

Sleet was falling through the bare trees and sliding down the metal roofs of the headquarters' buildings. It stuck to the places on Lovie's face that Dingo had licked. She rolled over on her stomach and was soothed by the slow rhythmic clanking of the windmill. But she was about to become permanently affixed to the ice castle forming around her from the water trickling over the side of the drinking tub.

She scooched to her hands and knees and looked around. A beam of light moved slowly across the thicket where the cows were bedded down. As the light passed from cow to cow, they blinked and stopped chewing their cuds momentarily. Vapor rose from the hair on their backs and puffed from their nostrils.

The light found Lovie's face and blinded her. "Oh-h-h," she moaned. Her head throbbed. Dingo came back and gave her a kiss on the mouth.

"Lovie!" her mother shouted. "Thank goodness I've found you! What are you doing out here?" At Mrs. Grady's raised voice, Dingo slinked away into the darkness.

Mrs. Grady helped her daughter to her feet and hugged her warmly.

"You scared me to death. Your dad and I have been worried sick. I thought I told you not to come out here."

"I'm sorry, Mom. I really am. But there wasn't any firewood in the courtyard. Then the electricity went out so I took the wheelbarrow to the thicket to get some but I...I don't know what I did with it."

"Lovie, are you alright? We have plenty of wood. Let's get you inside by the fire. You're just about frozen stiff." Mrs. Grady led Lovie through the ice-covered grape arbor and shined the flashlight at the potting shed. The wheelbarrow overflowed with firewood. "Look. We have more than plenty. The potting shed is stacked full too. We have enough wood to keep us warm if our electricity doesn't come back on until June."

Golden firelight streamed out of the sliding glass doors of Grampa Hank's den. Mrs. Grady slid open the door and Lovie's cold face and hands felt the warm blast of air from inside. Arm in arm, mother and daughter stood silently by the fireplace for a moment, savoring its warmth together.

"Mom? Did you build this fire?"

"Very funny. I only wish I could build a 'mantle melter' like this. You and Grampa Hank are the only ones who could ever build a fire like this—and I thank you for it. It was so nice to be able to bring my afghan in here and warm up after the electricity went out."

Lovie closed her eyes against the brightness of the crackling fire and turned her back to it. "Do we have any headache medicine, Mom? I think I have a concussion. Would you look at my eyes?"

"A concussion? Sit down on the couch and tell me what happened to you out there?"

"Okay. Um...I don't really know. I remember bumping into the windmill tower in the dark and I remember the dogs chasing a skunk. But I don't remember building this fire."

"You don't? Well let me have a look." Lovie grimaced when her mother shined the flashlight in her eyes. "Lovie...I can't see your eyes with them closed. Try to open them. I do see you have quite a bruise on your forehead though. And your neck is cut. You must've tangled with a mesquite branch. And you must've leaned too close to the fireplace when you built the fire because your eyebrows look singed. But your eyes look just fine—pretty and green as ever. You need to realize what a pretty girl you are and stop stewing about your hair and braces all the time. I think your naturally curly hair is spectacular. Mine is so limp I can hardly do anything with it."

Lovie smiled, without even thinking of hiding the green and red rubber bands on her teeth. "Thanks, Mom. I'm really, really sorry I got so mad at you about selling all the cattle."

"Actually, I didn't sell them all. The deal with the Mexican buyer fell through because the port of entry is closed for who knows how long. So we still have a few cows. And the strangest thing happened. Somehow the day workers left one of the yearling bulls in the thicket, so he didn't sell either. I saw him out there when I was looking for you. He's probably the best yearling of the bunch, too."

Dingo scratched on the sliding glass door. He drooped his ears as far as he could droop them and whined his most pitiful whine.

"Can't we please let him in, Mom, just for tonight?"

"Maybe so. But you said the dogs were chasing a skunk. Let me go see if he smells like a skunk first." Mrs. Grady slid open the door a few inches to take a sniff of the dog, but he squeezed inside without giving her the chance.

He leapt onto the couch beside Lovie with his dirty wet feet. She pushed him off and spread out her slicker on the floor and patted a spot in the middle. Dingo turned around twice, dropped down and began licking his feet. Lovie curled up on the couch then reached down and stroked his head. "He just smells like a wet dog, Mom."

Before closing the door, Mrs. Grady shined the flashlight around the courtyard. "I'm worried about Cotton. She's been moving so slowly lately. When I was in the thicket, I called her and called her but she never came. I'm afraid she might've confronted whatever was howling out there. I have to admit it sounded just like a wolf."

Dingo suddenly felt the need to be closer to Lovie. He crawled back onto the couch and settled in the crook of her knees. The contents of one of her jeans' pockets poked her so she got up and emptied it out onto the coffee table. Something on the table sparkled in the firelight.

Mrs. Grady lunged to scoop it up. Dingo dived off the couch and hid under Granny's grand piano. "Lovie! You found my bracelet! Thank you! Thank you! I dreaded telling your dad I lost it. He'd have been crushed. He had Granny's jeweler make it especially for me." She fastened the bracelet around her wrist and clutched her hand over it. "Where on earth did you find it?"

"I don't remember."

"You don't? You really must've whacked your head a good one."

"I did. I think I cuckooed myself. I've heard of people seeing stars, but I saw peacocks and ostriches and a big gray horse."

The color drained from Mrs. Grady's face. She picked up her afghan from the arm of a chair and wrapped it around herself. She backed up so close to the fireplace, Lovie was afraid the afghan would catch fire.

"The only gray horse that's ever been on this ranch is the one El Lobo lost in the flood I was telling you about. But you don't have to worry about him bothering you anymore, Lovie. The sheriff called earlier to tell me El Lobo stole one of our ranch pickups and was involved in a head-on collision on the ice on the highway bridge. He crashed over the side and probably drowned in the river—a fitting end if you ask me. They pulled the pickup out but he wasn't in it. They'll look for his body again when it gets light. The bad thing is that the local grocer and his little son and daughter were in the other vehicle. They were killed instantly."

Mrs. Grady turned and faced the fire. "I know I shouldn't have kept all that about El Lobo and his family a secret but it was just so unpleasant—and I was ashamed. His wife, Maria, used to be a good friend of mine, but I wasn't a very good friend of hers. And now it's too late to tell her I'm sorry. I was even jealous that Granny loved Maria's little girl so much. Granny never quit wishing she could've watched Angela grow up."

Memories held Mrs. Grady captive for awhile. Then she shook them off and turned back around with a smile on her face. "Lovie, your dad made arrangements for us all to go skiing at Angel Fire over New Year's. I know it'll be sad for you not to spend your whole Christmas vacation at the ranch but there's nothing to keep us here right now and Mr. Upchurch offered to send somebody over to take care of the rest of the cattle since the Mexico deal is off."

"Who's Mr. Upchurch?"

"P.D. Upchurch. He was one of Grampa Hank's dearest friends. His ranch is just down the river. He knows what a turmoil it is to lose a family member. He lost his oldest son, Pete Jr., in a jeep accident a couple of years ago. It was tragic. The boy had so much potential."

Mrs. Grady reached for her daughter's hands and squeezed them. "Believe me, Lovie, I know it's been hard for you to lose Grampa Hank so soon after losing Granny and possibly to lose the ranch that was so much a part of him. The Crossover Ranch is a dream you both shared. I know that. But my history with the ranch is different than yours and so are my feelings for it. Your dad and I have our own dreams. Please try to understand that."

"I think I do understand that now, Mom. I don't know how I do, but I do. Maybe I got some sense knocked into me when I butted heads with the windmill. I'm sorry for being so selfish before. It's just so sad when people you love cross over."

"Cross over? Where did you hear that term? Maybe a miracle will happen. Maybe Grampa Hank actually did do some estate planning and we'll find his will and the Crossover Ranch can be yours without the death tax tearing it totally apart. Just think; maybe someday you can give Granny's 'follow your dreams' speech to your own grandkids."

The electricity flickered and the piano light came back on. Dingo looked sheepish when it revealed his whereabouts, but when no one seemed to mind him being there he yawned and curled back up into a ball.

Lovie yawned, too. "This is December 21st, right? It's the shortest day of the year. That makes it the longest night and I intend to take advantage of the rest of it. I'm going to bed."

"Sounds like a good plan to me. I want to get an early start on the ranch books in the morning so we can get home before Christmas. Can you believe Dad bought a live tree and decorated it for us?"

"Dad did? Awesome!" Lovie gave her mother a warm hug. Above the fireplace, the firelight twinkled in the buffalo head's glass eyes. "Merry Christmas, Mom."

"Merry Christmas, Lovie. Before you go upstairs, be sure to call Dad and tell him you're safe. And feed Dingo, please. He looks hungry as usual. You might put some out for Cotton, too. She's too old to have gone far. I have to put a load of clothes in the dryer before I go to bed. I washed my sale barn clothes before the power went out and I'm hoping the dryer still works. Somebody taped the door shut with duct tape of all things." Mrs. Grady threw off her afghan and knocked a kachina doll off the mantle.

Lovie watched Grampa Hank's wolf kachina tumble head over heels toward the roaring fire. It seemed to fall in slow motion but she could not make herself move a muscle to save it.

Mrs. Grady caught it just before it hit the hearth. "This old thing is heavier than it looks. I say we use it for a doorstop. The Crossover Ranch wouldn't be the same without a wolf at the door."